D0397021

DISNEY
The Never Girls

volume 1: books 1-3

Copyright © 2016 Disney Enterprises, Inc. All rights reserved. Published in the
United States by Random House Children's Books, a division of Penguin Random
House LLC, 1745 Broadway, New York, NY 10019, and in Canada by Penguin
Random House Canada Limited, Toronto, in conjunction with Disney Enterprises,
Inc. Random House and the colophon are registered trademarks and A STEPPING
STONE BOOK and the colophon are trademarks of Penguin Random House LLC.

The works in this collection were originally published separately in the United
States by Random House Children's Books as *In a Blink,* copyright © 2013 Disney
Enterprises, Inc., *The Space Between,* copyright © 2013 Disney Enterprises, Inc., and
A Dandelion Wish, copyright © 2013 Disney Enterprises, Inc. All rights reserved.

randomhousekids.com/disney
ISBN 978-0-7364-3580-2
Printed in the United States of America

10 9 8 7 6 5 4

Disney
The Never Girls

volume 1: books 1-3

Written by
Kiki Thorpe

Illustrated by
Jana Christy

A STEPPING STONE BOOK™

RANDOM HOUSE 🏠 NEW YORK

Never Land

Far away from the world we know, on the distant seas of dreams, lies an island called Never Land. It is a place full of magic, where mermaids sing, fairies play, and children never grow up. Adventures happen every day, and anything is possible.

There are two ways to reach Never Land. One is to find the island yourself. The other is for it to find you. Finding Never Land on your own takes a lot of luck and a pinch of fairy dust. Even then, you will only find the island if it wants to be found.

Every once in a while, Never Land drifts close to our world . . . so close a fairy's laugh slips through. And every once in an even longer while, Never Land opens its doors to a special few. Believing in magic and fairies from the bottom of your heart can make the extraordinary happen. If you suddenly hear tiny bells or feel a sea breeze where there is no sea, pay careful attention. Never Land may be close by. You could find yourself there in the blink of an eye.

One day, four special girls came to Never Land in just this way. This is their story.

Never Land

Pirate Cove

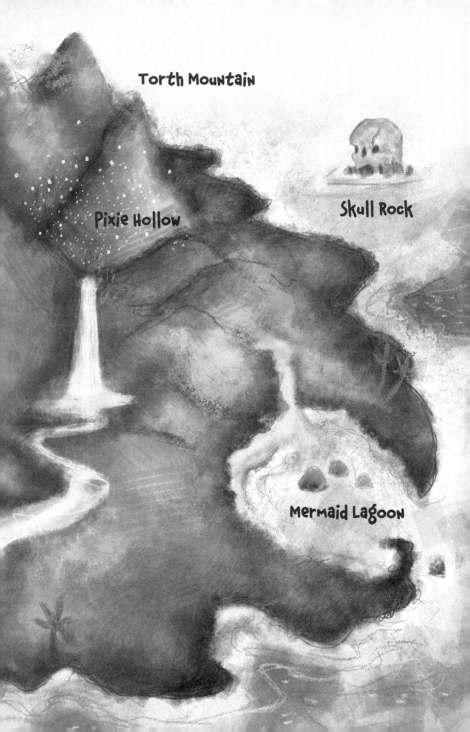

No one believed in fairies
more than Gabby.

The NeVeR GiRLs

in a blink

wRitteN by
Kiki Thorpe

IlluStrated by
JaNa ChriSty

A STEPPING STONE BOOK™

RANDOM HOUSE 🏠 NEW YORK

chapter 1

There it was. That sound again.

Kate McCrady froze. The soccer ball rolled past her, but she didn't even notice. She cocked her head to one side, listening.

Yes, it was the same sound she'd been hearing all afternoon. High and silvery, like little bells ringing. Kate looked around the backyard. What could it be?

"I got it!" yelled Lainey Winters. She chased the ball into the corner of the yard. Lainey's big glasses slid down her nose as she scooped up the ball. "I got it!" she cried again. "Kate's the monkey in the middle now!"

Across the lawn, Kate's best friend, Mia Vasquez, put her hands on her hips. "What's the matter, Kate?" she asked. It wasn't like Kate to miss such an easy pass.

"Do you hear that sound?" Kate asked her.

"What sound?" Mia replied.

"What's going on?" called Lainey, feeling left out. "Aren't we playing?"

Kate listened again. She couldn't hear the bells anymore. She felt excited, although she didn't know why. "It was nothing, I guess," she said, turning back to the game.

"You're in the middle now," Mia reminded her.

Kate shrugged. She was good at soccer. She was good at most things that involved running, jumping, kicking, or catching. She was never in the middle for very long.

"Okay, Lainey. You come take my spot," she called. "Lainey! Lainey?"

*

Lainey didn't hear her. She was staring up at the sky. A flock of flamingos was passing overhead.

Flamingos? thought Lainey. *That can't be right.* Lainey's third-grade science book had a picture of a flamingo in it. Flamingos lived in warm, sunny places. They lived near oceans and lakes. They didn't live in cities like Lainey's.

Maybe her glasses were playing tricks on her. Lainey took them off and rubbed

them on her shirt. When she put them back on, the flamingos were gone. Where they'd been, Lainey saw only feathery clouds.

"Lainey!" Mia yelled.

Lainey looked over, startled. "Did you see the flamingos?" she asked.

From the way Kate and Mia stared at her, Lainey could tell she'd said something wrong. She felt her face turn red.

"We're ready to play," said Kate. "But you have the ball."

Lainey looked down at the ball in her arms. "Oh, right." Lainey set the ball down on the grass. She glanced up at the sky one last time. Not a flamingo in sight.

But as the clouds drifted toward the horizon, Lainey could have sworn she heard the sound of flapping wings.

✷

Across the lawn, Mia was growing impatient. Why were her friends acting so funny today? All Mia wanted to do was finish their game!

At last, to Mia's relief, Lainey kicked the ball. *Good,* Mia thought. *No more interruptions.*

But just then the back door of Mia's house slammed open. A small girl in a pink tutu burst outside. She went streaking across the lawn, making a noise like a bumblebee.

"Gabby!" Mia shouted at her little sister. She was headed right for Kate, who was chasing the ball. "Watch out!"

Too late! Gabby slammed into Kate. Both girls tumbled to the ground.

"Gabby!" Mia hollered again, annoyed. "Quit getting in the way."

Gabby sat up. She straightened the costume fairy wings she was wearing. "I wasn't getting in the way," she said. "Kate got in *my* way. I was *flying*."

"You were not flying," Mia said. "You were being a pest."

"It's okay," said Kate, getting up from the grass. "Gabby, do you want to play with us?"

"Yes!" said Gabby at the same moment that Mia said, "No!"

The two sisters glared at each other. "Gabby, you're too little," Mia said in her best big-sister voice. "Go play somewhere else."

Gabby stuck her tongue out at Mia. Then she stomped off toward the flower bed. Gabby liked to play among the flowers, even though she wasn't supposed to.

"Gabby, you leave Mami's flowers alone," Mia said.

Gabby ignored her. She crouched down and examined something in the tulips. "Ooh!" she exclaimed. "A fairy!"

Mia rolled her eyes. Her little sister had a big imagination. But at least she wasn't bugging them anymore. Mia turned back to the game.

At that moment, the wind picked up. Mia caught the smell of seawater. *That's odd*, she thought. She looked around. Something about the way the breeze was blowing made the scrawny trees in her yard sound like rustling palms. Mia had the funny feeling that if she peeked through the fence, she would see the ocean right next door.

Of course, she knew that was crazy.

The ocean was hundreds of miles away.

The wind sent the soccer ball sailing into a corner of the yard. It bent the flowers on their stems and whipped the girls' hair. Above it, Mia could hear a noise like waves crashing on a beach.

The other girls heard it, too. Something strange was happening. They stepped closer together and reached for each other's hands.

"Gabby?" Mia cried, suddenly afraid. "Gabby, come here!"

*

When the fairy appeared in the garden, Gabby was not surprised. She often pretended to talk to fairies. Sometimes she pretended she *was* a fairy. Fairies were so much a part of Gabby's world that it seemed perfectly natural to see one sitting among her mother's tulips.

"Hello, fairy," Gabby said.

"I'm Prilla," said the fairy. "Clap if you believe in fairies!"

No one believed more than Gabby. She clapped her hands hard. Prilla the fairy turned a happy cartwheel in the air.

"I have to go home now," said Prilla.

"Don't go yet!" Gabby cried, just as the wind started to pick up.

The wind was blowing hard. Gabby heard her sister calling, "Gabby? Gabby, come here!"

Because she was afraid Prilla might blow away, Gabby put her hands around her. She held the fairy lightly, cupped in her palms, the way you would hold a butterfly.

And then Mia grabbed her.

The moment Mia touched Gabby, the world blinked. All the girls felt it. It was like the slow click of a camera lens.

The next instant, the backyard was gone.

chapter 2

The girls were standing on an empty beach. Where the fence had been a moment before, waves now curled against a sandy shore. Instead of a house, behind them rose a wall of dense green forest.

A rustling overhead made them look up. A flock of pink flamingos was crossing the sky.

"I *did* see flamingos," Lainey murmured.

"Are we dreaming?" asked Mia.

Kate didn't think it was a dream. She'd

never had a dream so sharp and so clear. But just to be sure, she reached out and pinched Mia.

"Ow!" Mia rubbed her arm. *"Kate!"*

Kate grinned. "I guess we're not dreaming."

"Mia," Gabby complained, "you're squeezing too hard."

Mia let go of Gabby's arm, which she'd been gripping tightly. Then she noticed Gabby's cupped palms. "What have you got in your hands?" Mia asked.

"A fairy," said Gabby.

"Gabby," said Mia, giving her sister a stern look. "What's the rule about fibbing?"

"But I *do* have a fairy. See?" Gabby opened her hands. A real, live fairy flew out.

The other girls jumped back, startled.

"Oh my gosh!" Mia gasped.

The fairy had curly brown hair and a lemon-yellow glow. She looked as surprised to see the girls as they were to see her. She blinked three times. Then, quick as a wink, she darted away.

"Come back!" Gabby cried.

But the fairy didn't stop. They could see her glow zigzagging between the trees.

Kate turned to her friends. "Well, don't just stand there!" Her heart was pounding with excitement. "Let's follow her!"

*

Prilla raced toward Pixie Hollow, flying as fast as her wings would carry her. Right then she would have given anything to be a fast-flying-talent fairy.

Of course, Prilla thought unhappily, *if I*

were *a fast-flying-talent fairy, I wouldn't be in this mess.*

She rounded a clump of wildflowers and Tinker Bell's workshop came into view. If anyone could help her, it was Tink.

When Prilla burst through the door of the workshop, Tink looked up with a frown. She didn't like to be interrupted while she was working on her pots and pans. But she saw the look on Prilla's face and put down the saucepan she was fixing. "What's wrong?" she asked.

"A problem," Prilla replied. "A big, *big* problem!"

"Well, bring it to me," said Tink. "Whatever it is, I'm sure I can fix it."

"I can't bring it here." Prilla wrung her hands. "Can you come with me?"

"Now?" Tink glanced down at her saucepan. "I was just in the middle of—"

"It's an emergency!" Prilla begged.

Tink sighed. "All right," she said. "What *is* the problem, anyway?"

"I think you need to see this for yourself," said Prilla. Grabbing Tink's hand, she pulled her out the door.

When they reached the beach, Prilla

stopped and hovered in the air. "They were here when I left!" she cried.

"*They?*" asked Tink.

From far off, the fairies heard a shout. Tink's pointed ears pricked up. "That sounds like Clumsies!"

"That's what I wanted to show you," said Prilla. "Come on."

Prilla and Tink followed the voices into the forest. And then Tink got her first look at Prilla's problem.

Or four problems, to be exact. Four girls were making their way through the trees. The tallest one led the way. She had freckles, a mop of red hair, and a bouncy walk. The girl walking behind her had big glasses that kept sliding down her nose. A girl with long, curly black hair brought up the rear. She held the hand of

a little girl who looked as if she might be her sister. The little girl kept pulling her hand away.

Tink stared. The littlest girl had wings. Tink had never seen a Clumsy with wings before.

"Kate," the girl with glasses said hesitantly, "do you think maybe we're lost?"

The red-haired girl stopped. She put her hands on her hips and looked around. "How can we be lost when we don't even know where we are?" she asked.

"I've never seen these Clumsies before," Tink whispered to Prilla. "Where did they come from?"

"Um . . . ," Prilla said, squirming a little. "Well, you see, I brought them."

"What?" Tink was so shocked her

wings missed a beat. She dropped an inch in the air.

"I didn't mean to," Prilla said quickly. "It was an accident."

Tink pulled on her bangs, as she always did when she was annoyed or confused. Right now, she was both. "Maybe you'd better start from the beginning."

"I was on a blink," Prilla explained. Prilla had an unusual talent, even for a fairy. She could visit children anywhere in the world just by blinking. Prilla's talent was very important. By visiting children, she helped keep their belief in fairies alive. And fairies thrived through children's belief.

Tink nodded. "Go on."

"It was like any other blink, until I

tried to come back," Prilla said. "When I got to Never Land, the girls were here, too! I must have brought them with me!"

"Well, then just blink them back to wherever they came from," said Tink, crossing her arms.

"I tried!" Prilla said. "It didn't work. Oh, Tink, what should I do?"

Tink sighed. This was the trouble with being a fairy who fixed things. Other fairies came to her with all kinds of problems, and not all of them involved pots and pans.

At that moment, the little girl looked up and spotted them. "My fairy's back!" she cried.

"She brought a friend!" the one with glasses said.

The girls scrambled to get a closer look.

"Ooh! See her tiny ponytail?"

"And her little leaf-dress?"

"Look at the pom-poms on her shoes."

"She's sooo cute!"

"I'm not cute!" Tink exclaimed.

Tink had never been very fond of Clumsies (except for Peter Pan, of course), and these girls seemed like a particularly silly bunch. "Prilla, these girls don't belong in Pixie Hollow. Send them home."

"But Tink . . . ," Prilla began.

Just then, they heard the whisper of wings. A third fairy appeared in the glen. It was Spring, a messenger. Prilla and Tink flew over to her.

"Come to the Home Tree at once," Spring told them.

"What is it?" Prilla asked, her heart sinking.

Spring glanced at the four girls. "Bring your Clumsies. The queen wants to have a word with you."

chapter 3

As the three fairies flew off, Kate scrambled after them. "Quick!" she cried. "Don't let them get away this time!"

The girls chased the fairies through the forest. They ducked under branches. They climbed over fallen logs. They hadn't heard Spring's message and didn't realize that the fairies *wanted* them to follow.

"Where do you think we're going?" Lainey asked, panting a little. The trees were starting to thin out. They could see blue sky up ahead.

"I don't know," Kate said. "But I—"

As Kate stepped into the clearing, her words died on her lips. The other girls came up behind her. They, too, fell silent in wonder.

To understand what the girls felt when they first saw Pixie Hollow, think of your most marvelous dream. Maybe it was filled with soft sunlight or beautiful music or the smell of orange blossoms. Maybe you discovered hidden treasure. Maybe everything felt possible.

For the girls, Pixie Hollow was all those things and more. They were standing at the edge of a meadow thick with wildflowers. And everywhere they looked, they saw fairies.

A fairy rode
past on the back
of a jackrabbit.
Another
wove
through
the air
chasing a
bright blue
butterfly. Fairies
darted in and out among
the flowers. Their wings
sparkled in the sunlight.

Kate started to step forward. Then she
drew her foot back with a gasp. A fairy
was crossing the ground in front of her.
He was riding in a little cart pulled by a
mouse. When he saw Kate, he almost fell
off his seat in surprise.

The girls made their way slowly through the meadow, being careful where they stepped. Fairies in flower-petal dresses buzzed around them. Soon the girls had drawn a crowd. The fairies kept repeating the same word—"Clumsy."

"Why do they keep saying that?" Mia wondered.

"Maybe they're talking about you," Kate teased.

"I'm not clumsy!" Mia said, offended. She turned to the nearest fairy, saying, "I've had three years of ballet!" The fairy darted away in alarm.

"Oh!" Kate stopped walking so suddenly that the other girls bumped into her. "Look at *that*!"

Ahead stood a maple tree as big as a house. Looking closer, the girls saw that it *was* a house. Tiny doors and windows lined its branches. Several of the windows flew open. Fairies stuck their heads out to stare at the girls.

"Come on! Come on!" The fairies they had been following beckoned to them.

At the base of the great tree was a pebbled courtyard. A fairy stood in the center of it. She wore a long gown made of rose petals. A thin band of gold rested on her head.

"She must be a queen," Mia whispered.

Kate had been leading the way. But now, for the first time, she hesitated. She had never met a queen before. She wasn't sure what to do.

To Kate's astonishment, Gabby stepped in front of her. The little girl held the edges of her tutu and curtsied.

The queen looked pleased. "I am Queen Clarion," she said in a voice that seemed to belong to someone much bigger. "Tell me, why have you come here?"

At last, Kate found her voice. "Your Majesty," she said, stepping forward, "we don't know why we're here. We don't even know *where* we are."

The crowd of fairies tittered. Even the queen seemed surprised. "Why, you're in Pixie Hollow! On the island of Never Land. Are you saying you didn't mean to come?"

"It's my fault." A fairy fluttered forward. It was the one the girls had first seen on the beach.

"Go ahead, Prilla," the queen said.

Prilla explained to the queen what had happened with her blink. "I didn't mean to bring them. I'd fly backward if I could," Prilla added. She was afraid the queen would be angry. No fairy had ever blinked Clumsies to Never Land before.

The queen was quiet for a moment, thinking. "It seems these girls have come here by accident," she said at last. "All the same, we must find a way to get them home. Until then, they will be our guests. Fairies of Pixie Hollow, treat these Clumsies kindly."

"I'm *not* clumsy." Mia spoke up suddenly. "I'm Mia!"

Everyone turned to look at her. Mia blushed, but continued, "That's Kate, and that's Lainey. And this is my little sister, Gabby. We're not clumsy, and I wish you'd stop calling us that . . . er, Your Majesty." She added the last part to be polite.

Silence fell over the courtyard. The queen stared at Mia. Then she laughed. Her laugh was clear and bell-like. As soon as they heard it, the girls relaxed.

"Clumsies are what we call the people of the mainland—*your* world," Queen Clarion explained. "But you're right. While you're our guests, you should be called by your names. Mia, Kate, Lainey, and Gabby, welcome to Pixie Hollow."

The queen clapped her hands. A door in the side of the tree opened and dozens of fairies came out. They were all carrying food—whole strawberries, roasted walnuts, wheels of cheese the size of a penny, loaves of bread no bigger than your thumb . . . and last but not least, four beautiful cakes. It took two fairies each to carry them, although to the girls they were the size of cupcakes.

More fairies unrolled banana leaves to be used as the girls' place mats. Then Kate, Lainey, Mia, and Gabby sat down to their first fairy feast.

Tinker Bell had been watching from the edge of the courtyard. When the girls began to eat, she rose into the air.

Everything was settled. She could get back to her workshop now.

But as she turned to leave, the queen called to her. Tink flew over. "Yes, Queen Clarion?"

"We've never had so many Clumsies in Pixie Hollow," Queen Clarion said.

"No, we haven't," said Tink.

"Taking care of four girls won't be easy, will it?" the queen asked.

"I suppose not," Tink said absently. She was already thinking about her saucepan.

But the queen's next words got her attention. "I want you to help Prilla," the queen told Tink. "For the time being, it will be your job to look after the girls."

Chapter 4

Oh, the unfairness! As soon as she was alone, Tink stomped her tiny foot in the air. Somehow she'd gotten stuck with the Clumsies. Tink would rather have had her wings dipped in mud!

"Why me?" she grumbled to herself. "Any other fairy would do just fine." But what could she do? It was the queen's command. So when Prilla decided to give the girls a tour, Tink had no choice but to follow along.

Prilla started her tour with the Home Tree, as any fairy would. The Home Tree was the heart of the fairies' world.

Earlier, the girls had been too excited to examine the tree properly. But now they saw all the details they'd missed. They marveled at the great knothole door, the sea-glass windows, and the tiny steps that wound around the trunk.

"Where do those go?" Gabby pointed to the different colored doors lining the tree's great branches. Some had crystal doorknobs or dandelion doormats. Others had silver wind chimes or sea-fan awnings hung above them.

"To the fairies' rooms. Each room is decorated according to its fairy's talent," Prilla explained.

"What kind of talent?" asked Lainey.

"Every kind!" said Prilla. "Every fairy in Pixie Hollow has a talent. It's the thing she does best and loves to do more than anything else. Look, there in the courtyard, that's a sweeping-talent fairy. And the one over there, carrying that plum—that's a harvest-talent fairy."

Kate giggled. *What funny talents!* she thought. "If I were a fairy, I'd have an exciting talent," she whispered to Mia.

Mia nodded. She was busy peering into the windows of the tearoom. Kate peeked over her shoulder. She saw a table made from the polished cross section of a tree trunk. It was set with plates and cups made from seashells. The napkins were folded flower petals.

"Everything is so pretty! I wish I could shrink myself and go inside," Mia said.

"Over here is Tink's workshop," Prilla said, leading the girls around the side of the tree.

Tink, who'd been sulking behind a tree root, looked up with a start. Her workshop was her pride and joy. She didn't want Clumsies poking around in there! She hurried over to keep an eye on them.

When Gabby saw Tink's workshop, she squealed with delight. "It's a teakettle!" she exclaimed. Sure enough, a real, human-sized teakettle had been squeezed between the Home Tree's roots. Its spout made a little awning over the tiny door.

"Tink's a tinker-talent fairy," Prilla explained. "The best in Pixie Hollow."

Normally, Tink would have been pleased by the compliment. But she was too busy watching Mia. The girl was down on her hands and knees, peeking in the window.

"Oh, look!" Mia cried. "There's a teeny-tiny workbench. And a bucket made from a thimble. Oh! And look at that chair made from an old bent spoon!"

"Let me see! Let me see!" cried Gabby, tugging at Mia's sleeve.

The other girls took turns peeping inside. They were so enthusiastic that finally even Tink had to smile.

"Isn't it just the cutest thing you've ever seen?" Mia exclaimed.

Tink's smile faded. Prilla looked embarrassed.

"What's wrong?" asked Mia.

"Fairies don't like to be called cute," Prilla said. "It's insulting."

"Oh, I didn't know. I'm sorry, Miss Tink," Mia said. Tink just rolled her eyes.

"Fairies don't say 'sorry,'" Prilla told Mia. "They say, 'I'd fly backward if I could.'"

Mia glanced at Tink and nodded, clearly afraid to say anything else at all.

"It's okay," Prilla said kindly. "When I

first got here, I didn't understand all the rules, either."

"What other rules are there?" Lainey asked.

"Well, for starters, fairies don't say Mister or Miss," Prilla explained. "And be careful who you tell secrets to. Fairies love to gossip! And another thing." Prilla lowered her voice. "Watch out for Vidia, the fast-flying-talent fairy. . . ."

Prilla kept talking, but Kate wasn't listening anymore. Rules had always bored her.

Kate looked around for something interesting. She spied a little building made of twigs. It had a straw roof and a wide door.

"What's this?" Kate asked, striding

over to it. She bent down to open the door.

"Don't!" cried Tink. "That's the—"

Frightened squeaks drowned out the rest of her words. A dozen mice burst through the door. They ran off in every direction.

"Oopsie," said Kate.

"That's the dairy mouse barn," Tink finished with a sigh.

"I'll help!" cried Lainey. She started

to chase after the mice. But she only frightened them more.

A fairy flew out of the barn. "You clumsy Clumsies!" she yelled.

"Maybe we'd better move on," Prilla said quickly, and hurried the girls away. When Kate glanced back over her shoulder, she saw the fairy herding the mice back into the barn.

Prilla led the girls through Pixie Hollow. They saw garden fairies watering flowers and caterpillar-shearing-talent fairies herding woolly caterpillars. Two fairies riding on the backs of squirrels chased each other through the trees.

"What are they doing?" asked Lainey.

"Playing tag," Prilla replied. "Those are animal-talent fairies."

Tink and Prilla took the girls to the

orchard, where the harvest-talent fairies gave them just-picked peaches still warm from the sun. Next, they visited Havendish Stream. The girls watched the water-talent fairies sailing their leaf-boats.

Nearby, Kate saw a funny round building. It was built from odd little rocks. Going closer, she saw that they weren't rocks, but peach pits.

"What's this place?" she asked.

"The mill," Prilla said, flying over. "It's where we keep the fairy dust."

"What's fairy dust?" asked Lainey.

"It's what makes us sparkle," said a voice nearby.

A sparrow man flew around the side

of the mill. He had floppy blond hair and a friendly smile. "The dust also helps us fly," he told the girls. "Without it, we can't fly more than a foot at a time."

"This is Terence," Prilla told the girls. "He's a dust talent."

"Would you like to see inside?" Terence asked them.

The girls crowded around the double doors. In the dim light, they could see a dozen pumpkin-canisters.

Terence lifted the lid off one of the pumpkins. The fairy dust was finer than flour. It shimmered with the colors of the rainbow.

"That's a lot of dust," Mia said.

"It's just enough," Terence replied. "In Pixie Hollow there's just enough of everything. No more, no less."

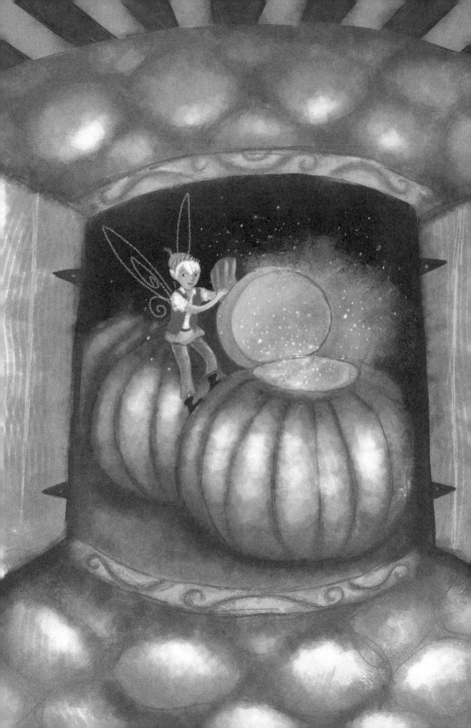

Kate was thinking about something Terence had said. "Fairy dust helps you fly. Could it help *us* fly, too?" she asked.

"Of course," Terence said. "Anyone can fly with fairy dust. In fact, that's how children usually get to Never Land. You're the first ones I've met to come on a blink."

Kate was startled by this news. "You mean, other kids have been here, too?"

"Oh, sure," said Terence. "Not very often, mind you. And usually they end up in other parts of Never Land. We don't see too many Clumsies in Pixie Hollow."

"So where are the kids now?" Mia wondered.

"Home," Tink said. The girls turned to her in surprise. It was the first time she'd spoken since the trouble at the mouse barn.

"Clumsies go home," Tink said again, matter-of-factly. "Unless they have no homes to go back to. Then they stay lost in Never Land forever."

The way she said "forever" sent a shiver down Kate's spine. "But," she said, "the ones who *do* go home, they come back to visit sometimes, don't they?"

"No, they don't," Tink said with a shrug. "They go home and grow up. And when they grow up, they forget. Never Land seems like something they once dreamed."

The girls were quiet, thinking about this. It was hard for them to imagine ever forgetting such a wonderful place.

"It's getting late," Prilla said, glancing at the sun. "We can see more of Pixie Hollow tomorrow."

"Come visit anytime," Terence told the girls as he shut the doors of the mill.

The setting sun turned the meadow gold as they made their way back to the Home Tree. It looked even more beautiful than when they'd first arrived in Pixie Hollow. But Kate barely saw it. Tink's words still troubled her.

Was it true that they would go home and forget about Never Land . . . or else stay here forever? To Kate, the choice—if it was a choice at all—seemed deeply unfair.

Well, I won't think about it, Kate told herself. After all, they were here now. There was still so much to do and see and discover.

Pushing the thought from her mind, Kate skipped ahead to join her friends.

chapter 5

"I can show you your room now," Prilla told the girls when they returned from the dust mill.

"We have a room?" Kate asked, surprised.

"Of course!" Prilla laughed. "Where did you think you'd sleep? On the ground?"

Kate wouldn't have minded. Sleeping outside, with nothing but the stars overhead, was something she'd always wanted to try.

"Come on," said Prilla, "the decorating-talent fairies are almost finished."

The last bit of light was draining from the sky. Kate, Mia, Lainey, and Gabby followed the fairies to a large weeping willow. Light shone beneath the willow's leaves, as if the tree glowed from within.

Tinker Bell parted the branches, and the girls stepped inside.

Kate gasped. It was the perfect room. Four girl-sized hammocks hung from the tree's branches. The willow's leaves spilled down around them like curtains. The velvety grass had been raked into pretty spiral patterns. Soft light came from lanterns set into notches in the tree's trunk.

Gabby looked closer at one of the lanterns. Half a dozen fireflies circled inside. "Lightning-bug lights!" she cried.

Mia sank down into one of the hammocks. It had been filled with moss and covered with silk sheets to make a sort of swinging bed. She lifted a pillow to her face and sniffed. "It smells like roses."

"It's stuffed with rose petals," Prilla said. "Do you like it?"

"It's the most beautiful room I've ever seen," Mia replied.

The girls noticed two tiny hammocks hanging next to theirs. "Do you live here, too?" Gabby asked the fairies hopefully.

"Tink and I have our own rooms in the Home Tree," Prilla explained. "But we thought we should stay with you, for now, anyway."

On another branch, Lainey discovered

a basin made from tightly woven banana leaves. It was filled with cool springwater. The girls washed their faces, and cleaned their teeth with licorice twigs. The sewing-talent fairies had made nightgowns for them by stitching together flannel sheets. The girls slipped these over their heads, shivering at the softness.

As they climbed into their beds, Tink went around tapping the lanterns to put the fireflies out.

"Leave one on," Mia said. "At home, Mami always leaves a light on for Gabby."

"Oh!" Lainey gasped and sat up. "Home!"

Until that moment, the girls had not

thought once of their parents. But now, as if waking from a dream, they realized how long they'd been gone.

"Our moms and dads are going to be so worried!" said Mia.

"They're going to be so *angry*," Kate added grimly.

"If only there were a way we could send a message. Just to let them know we're all right," said Lainey.

Tink, who was examining Gabby's wings, looked up. "Prilla could take a note," she said.

"That's right—I could blink there! Oh, Tink, you're so clever," said Prilla.

Tink shrugged and turned back to the wings. She had been alarmed when Gabby took them off and hung them on a twig. But now she saw that they were made of cloth and wire. Not real fairy wings at all.

The girls got busy preparing their message. Kate declared that Mia should write it, since she had the best handwriting. The fairies had no pens or paper. Mia wrote on a strip of birch bark using a twig dipped in berry ink.

Dear Mami and Papi,
How are you? We are fine. We are
Visiting in Never Land. It's nice here.
Please tell the other moms don't worry.
Love, Mia Gabby Lainey Kate

Mia fanned the wet ink. When it was dry, she gave the note to Prilla. Prilla held the rolled-up bark in her arms. She pictured a tunnel with Mia and Gabby's house at the end of it.

She blinked.

Prilla was in a dark room. She could hear soft snores. Looking down, she saw a sleeping boy holding a stuffed dinosaur.

Wrong house! Prilla blinked again.

She was sitting on the pages of an open book. A boy and a girl stared down at her. "Look, Mom! A fairy!" cried the girl.

"No, it's a picture of a bird. See?" Their mother's finger landed on the page next to Prilla. She blinked away.

On her third blink, Prilla found herself on the doorstep of a narrow brick house. It looked like Mia and Gabby's house, as far as Prilla could remember. Prilla placed the note on the doorstep. Then she blinked away—too soon to see the wind pick up the note and carry it off.

"I did it!" she exclaimed as she arrived
back in the willow room.

"Did what?" asked Kate.

"I delivered the note," Prilla said. "I
didn't mean to be gone so long. It took a
while to find the right house."

"But you've been right here the whole
time," said Kate. To the girls, no more
than an instant had passed. Prilla hadn't
even left the room.

Prilla was surprised to hear this. She had never thought about what a blink looked like from the other side.

"Do you think it might be like that for us?" Lainey asked after a moment. "Do you think back at home no time has passed since we left?"

Prilla considered Lainey's question. "Maybe so," she said. "A blink is a blink, whichever way you go."

A sigh of relief went around the room. As soon as they were sure their parents wouldn't be worried, the girls' mood lifted.

"This is like a sleepover!" said Lainey, snuggling under the covers.

"It's better," Mia said. "We can stay up all night if we want!"

But it had been a long day, full of

surprises. Soon enough, their giggles gave way to yawns. One by one, Gabby, Lainey, and Mia dropped off to sleep.

*

Kate lay awake for a long time. She was too excited to sleep. All her life she had secretly believed that something extraordinary would happen to her. Now it finally had, and she didn't want to miss a single moment.

When she was sure everyone else was asleep, Kate threw back the covers and crept out of bed. Standing on tiptoe, she peeped into Prilla's and Tink's hammocks. They were asleep, too.

Quietly, Kate parted the willow branches and stepped outside.

If Pixie Hollow was enchanting by day,

it was even more so at night. Lanterns glowed softly in the trees. A warm breeze stirred up the scent of jasmine.

Kate made her way toward the meadow, the grass deliciously cool under her bare feet. She threw her arms wide and spun with joy. Today had been marvelous. And who knew what tomorrow would bring? There were no parents or teachers here, no rules or restrictions. Nothing but days and days of adventure ahead . . .

A laugh rang out from the darkness. Kate looked around. "Who's there?" she whispered.

A cricket's chirp was the only reply.

A cloud crossed the moon. Kate shivered and wrapped her arms around herself. *I'm imagining things,* she thought.

But the night seemed darker now. Turning, Kate started quickly back to the willow, brushing past a primrose bush. In her hurry, she didn't notice the pair of eyes gleaming at her from within its branches.

Chapter 6

When the girls awoke the next morning, they found a basket of freshly baked muffins waiting for them outside the willow tree. Tucked inside the basket was a note from Queen Clarion.

The note was written in Leaf Lettering, the secret fairy alphabet. Tink read it for the girls. "'You're to come to the fairy circle this morning,'" Tink said. "The queen has news."

"The fairy circle!" Prilla exclaimed. "It must be something important."

After breakfast, Prilla and Tink led the way across the meadow. It was another sparkling day. The sky was robin's-egg blue, and the grass smelled fresh with dew. The girls laughed and chatted as they walked.

But when they reached a little clearing in the woods, they got quiet. Around a hawthorn tree, a ring of toadstools sprouted from the mossy ground. A hushed feeling hung in the air. The girls could tell it was a magical place.

Queen Clarion was seated on a snow-white toadstool. On either side of her sat a fairy.

"This is Rain, a weather-talent fairy," said Queen Clarion, introducing the fairy

on her left. "Rain knows all there is to know about the weather of Never Land. And this is Skye, a seeing talent." Queen Clarion nodded to the other fairy. "Skye can see things the rest of us can't. She and Rain have news about how you came to Never Land."

Rain stepped forward. "A southern puff was bellowing," she said. "Cold highwilds drove the isle mainlandish—"

"What she means," Skye broke in, "is that we think Never Land rode the waves all the way to your home."

"Waves? You mean like the ocean?" asked Kate. Skye nodded.

"But that's impossible," said Mia. "We don't live near an ocean."

"Nothing's impossible," Skye said. "The island does what it wants. We think it came so close to your world that it only took the tiniest tug to bring you here."

"My blink!" Prilla realized.

"Exactly," said Skye. "I want to show you something."

From behind a toadstool, she dragged out an old pair of spectacles. The lenses were foggy. The wire rims were bent. The glasses clearly had seen much better days.

"Glasses?" asked Kate. She had been expecting something more exciting.

"I found these washed up on the beach one day," Skye explained. "I fixed them with a little fairy magic. Step inside the fairy circle and try them on."

As usual, Kate stepped forward first.

She stood in the middle of the ring of toadstools. She put on the glasses. Instead of seeing the forest in front of her, she saw a familiar front door. "I can see my house!" she cried.

The other girls tried the glasses, too. They all saw their own homes. "But why does it look so misty?" Lainey asked.

"The glasses tell you how close to the mainland you are. The farther away you are, the harder it is to see," Skye said.

"When will we be close again?" Mia asked.

Rain held up something that looked like a pinwheel. It spun in the breeze. "Elephoons running north," she said, watching the wheel spin. "Could be as soon as sun-twixt."

"What she *means*," Skye said, "is that it might be very soon. Between the next sunrise and sunset, in fact." When the girls looked puzzled, she added, "Prilla can blink you home tomorrow."

"Tomorrow?" Tink said, perking up. That meant her days of Clumsy-sitting were almost over. She could go back to her workshop! Tink couldn't help herself—she clicked her heels with joy.

Kate looked around at her friends. Their unhappy faces mirrored what she was feeling. "But we just *got* here," she said. "Do we have to leave already?"

"It might be your only chance," said Skye. "We don't know when Never Land will drift that way again."

"Skye and Rain, you've been very helpful," Queen Clarion told them. The two fairies nodded to the queen. Then they flew away.

As the girls left the fairy circle, Kate felt as if she might cry. *It's not fair,* she thought. *We haven't even had an adventure yet.*

"Well, what would you like to do on your last day in Pixie Hollow?" Prilla asked. She tried to make her voice light, although she felt as sad as the girls did. She was sorry to see them go so soon.

"We could go blueberry picking? Or leaf-boat racing? Or maybe wild mushroom hunting?"

"Flying," Kate said. She hadn't even known she was going to say it. The word popped out of her mouth. But once it had, she knew it with all her heart. "I want to fly."

"Yes!" Mia agreed, her face brightening.

"I want to fly, too!" said Lainey.

"Me three!" said Gabby.

"Gabby, you're too little—" Mia began. But Gabby gave her such a glare that Mia shut her mouth.

"We want to learn to fly," Kate repeated. "All of us."

Prilla looked at Tink, who shrugged. "I don't see why not," Tink said. "I'll ask if Terence can spare some fairy dust."

All the girls cheered.

Kate cheered loudest of all, because a plan was starting to form in her mind. It was a crazy, brilliant plan—a plan for returning to Never Land.

chapter 7

For their flying lesson, Tink led the girls to a bend in the stream. The ground here was carpeted with soft moss. Tree branches formed a canopy overhead.

"It's a good place to learn," Tink said. "Plenty of branches to catch yourself on, and a nice soft landing."

Terence had come along with them and had brought a small sack of fairy dust. "Who's first?" he asked the girls.

"Me!" said Kate. She watched as Terence

measured out a tiny fairy cupful of dust. "That's all we get?" It didn't look like enough dust to make her fly. It hardly looked like enough to make her sneeze.

"Fairy dust is precious," Tink said. "Everyone gets a cupful a day. No more, no less. Hold your breath now. You don't want any blowing away."

Kate held her breath as Terence poured the dust over her. At once, she felt a tingle from the tips of her ears to her toes. It felt like warming up next to a fire after a day of playing in the snow. She flapped her arms, but nothing happened.

"Now what?" she asked.

"Patience," said Tink. Terence was pouring dust over the other girls.

"Ooh!" Prilla fluttered up and down. "This is so exciting!"

"Think of something light," Tink said. "Wriggle your shoulders. Bounce on your toes."

The girls concentrated. They wriggled. They bounced. And then . . .

"Oh my gosh!" Mia squealed. Her feet were leaving the ground. "Gabby, hold on!" Mia clutched her little sister's hand and together they rose into the air.

"Look at me! I'm flying!" Lainey cried, floating up next to them.

Kate still wasn't moving. She pushed off the ground—hard—and shot high into the air. "Hey! Look at meeee— Ow!" Kate bonked her head on a tree branch. Clutching her head, she sank back down to the ground.

"Meow?" Lainey giggled as she floated by. "You sound like a cat, Kate."

Kate scowled and rubbed her head. Gabby bobbed past, her wings fluttering in the breeze. "Come on, Kate. It's fun," she said. She turned a shaky somersault in the air. "Wheeeee!"

Kate pushed off again. But instead of going up, she went sideways. "Ooof!" she grunted as she hit a tree trunk. She landed on the ground again.

Above her, Mia was swimming gracefully through the air. Kate watched her jealously. Mia looked like a mermaid, with her long hair streaming out behind her.

Kate scowled. *Why can't I fly like that?* At home, she was usually the one who was good at things.

Maybe I'm not trying hard enough. Kate closed her eyes. She thought of light

things—feathers, clouds, dandelion fluff. She thought so hard she gave herself a headache.

"I can see the whole world!" Mia cried from somewhere above her.

Kate gritted her teeth. "Concentrate!" she told herself. She pushed off again. This time she rose higher . . . and higher. . . .

"I did it!" cried Kate. "I'm flying!"

She was headed right toward Mia. *Why is Mia holding on to that tree branch?* Kate wondered.

At the last second, Kate noticed Mia's pale face. She saw how tightly Mia was gripping the branch. She realized that Mia was terrified.

But it was too late. Kate couldn't stop. She crashed into Mia, who let go of the branch. They both screamed as they started to fall.

"Think of flying!" Tink shouted at them. *"Believe* you can fly!" But the girls couldn't think of anything but the ground speeding toward them.

Kate smacked into Lainey on the way down. Now all three were falling.

Splash!

Splash!

Splash!

One after another, the girls landed in Havendish Stream.

Gabby was still doing air-somersaults. But seeing the older girls fall, she fell, too. Gabby always wanted to do what the big kids did. She landed in the stream right next to Kate. *Splash!*

The girls were soaked. They were shivering. "Thanks a lot, Kate," Mia said through chattering teeth.

Just then, they heard a high, silvery sound, like little bells ringing. It was Tink laughing. The girls stared, astonished. They'd never heard Tink laugh before.

"I think," Tink said, wiping her eyes, "that's enough flying for one day."

*

Kate was quiet on the way back to Pixie Hollow. She walked slowly behind the other girls, thinking.

Terence had said that other kids had once flown to Never Land with Peter Pan. If that was true, Kate and her friends could fly there, too. That was Kate's plan— to come back to Never Land whenever she wished. Just because other kids hadn't come back didn't mean it wasn't possible.

For Kate's plan to work, though, she had to learn to fly. But she hadn't flown—not for more than a moment, anyway. Certainly not well enough to fly across an ocean.

And now it was too late. Tomorrow they had to go home and leave Pixie Hollow behind—maybe forever.

The more Kate thought, the more slowly she walked. The more slowly she walked, the more she fell behind. At some point, Kate realized she could no longer hear her friends' voices.

She stopped and looked around. She wasn't sure which way to go.

"Hello?" she called uncertainly. "Hey, guys?"

The leaves of a bush nearby rustled. Kate spun around. She remembered she was in a strange forest. Who knew what kind of creatures lived there?

Kate picked up a big stick. Holding it like a sword, she faced the bush.

Out flew a fairy.

Kate sighed, relieved. "Just a fairy!"

"Yes, clever one, I'm a fairy." The fairy had long black hair and a pale, pinched face. Her wings were narrow and pointed like knives. "Are you planning to bash me with that stick?" she asked Kate.

Kate lowered the stick. "What are you doing here?" she asked.

"I go where I please, darling," the fairy said with a sniff. "What are *you* doing here? And why are you all wet?"

Kate looked down at her damp clothes. "We had a flying lesson," she said. "It didn't go very well."

The fairy smirked. "Clumsies can't fly. They don't have wings!"

"My friends don't have wings and *they* flew," Kate pointed out.

"Is that so? Then I guess you simply have no talent," the fairy said.

"I guess not," Kate agreed sadly.

"Although, if you *really* want to fly, I might be able to help you," the fairy said.

"How?" asked Kate.

"Well, sweet, I *am* the best fast flier in Pixie Hollow." As if to prove it, the fairy buzzed a circle around Kate's head.

A flying-talent fairy! Kate's heartbeat quickened. She noticed how this fairy's wings sliced the air as she flew. Other fairies fluttered. "You'd really help me?" Kate asked.

"I could. Though I'd need your help in return," the fairy said slyly.

"Of course," Kate agreed.

"Then meet me at moonrise in the orchard. By the sour-plum tree." The fairy turned to leave.

"Wait!" Kate called. "What's your name?"

The fairy glanced back. "Vidia."

Somewhere in the back of Kate's mind, the name rang a bell. But she hadn't been listening when Prilla warned them about Vidia. "My name's Kate," she said.

Vidia shrugged as if Kate's name was not important. She started away.

"Oh! Wait!" Kate called. "How do I get back to . . ." She trailed off. Vidia was already gone.

Just then, Tink flew up. "There you are!" she cried when she saw Kate. "We've been looking for you." She looked around. "Who were you talking to?"

"It was—nothing. Nobody," said Kate. For some reason she didn't want to tell

Tink about her flying lesson with Vidia.

Tink's brow furrowed. But to Kate's relief, she didn't ask any more questions. "Well, come on, then," Tink said. "The other girls are waiting."

Even Tink's scowl didn't dampen Kate's spirits. She was going to learn to fly—from the fastest flier in Pixie Hollow!

Chapter 8

That night, after her friends fell asleep, Kate sneaked out of the willow room. At the edge of the orchard, she spotted a bent tree with twisted branches. Right away she knew it was the sour-plum tree.

"Vidia?" Kate whispered. A moment later, she felt a tiny breeze as Vidia flew up beside her.

"I'm ready for my flying lesson," Kate told her.

"First things first, dearest. We need fairy dust." Vidia held out something that resembled a man's sock.

Kate looked closer. It *was* a man's sock. It was long and red with a stitched-up hole in the toe. "I took it from a pirate," Vidia told her. "Don't worry, I washed it."

"What's it for?" asked Kate.

"To carry the dust, clever one! Now go ahead. Fill it up."

"The whole thing?" Kate was shocked. The sock was as long as her forearm. "Tink says everyone only gets a cupful."

Vidia smirked. "Tink doesn't care about flying. Not like *we* do."

"But—"

"Use your head, sweetness. If a tiny cup of dust helps you fly, think how much faster you'd go with more."

Kate took the sock. "Why can't you get the dust yourself?" she asked.

"Dearest, if we stand around talking all night long, there will be no time for flying," Vidia said. "Now off you go."

As Kate started away, Vidia added, "Don't worry, fairy dust belongs to us all."

Kate walked along the stream toward the mill. She felt funny. It didn't seem right to take fairy dust in the middle of the night. It seemed like stealing.

But Vidia said fairy dust belongs to everyone, Kate reminded herself. Besides, she would need extra fairy dust for all her friends to fly back to Never Land, too.

Ahead, in the moonlight, she could see

the mill. Kate tiptoed closer. She hoped Terence was there. Then she could just ask for the fairy dust.

"Hello?" Kate whispered. "Anyone here?"

The only sound was the *splish-splash* of the waterwheel turning in the stream.

Kate tried the big double doors. They opened easily. Through them, she could just make out the shapes of the pumpkin-canisters.

Kate was too big to crawl inside. But she could easily fit her arm through the door. She reached in and pulled a pumpkin toward her. Taking off its lid, she saw that it was three-quarters full. The dust glittered faintly in the moonlight.

Kate dipped her hand in and pulled

out a fistful . . . and another and another.
In the end, it took most of the dust in the
pumpkin to fill the sock.

Fairy dust belongs to everyone, Kate told
herself again. She put the canister back
and closed the doors.

As she stood, she noticed that her
hands were sparkly with dust. She could

feel its magic already starting. She half ran, half flew all the way to the sour-plum tree.

Vidia grinned when she saw the filled sock. She scooped out a big portion for herself, then one for Kate. When she was done, Kate tied the sock through a belt loop in her jeans.

"All right. Follow me," Vidia said, and dove into the air.

Kate sprang after her. The extra fairy dust made her feel powerful. In a flash, she was high above the sour-plum tree.

But a second later, she started to sink. She tried to think of light things, as Tink had told her to do. But the ground was coming fast. . . .

"You're trying too hard," Vidia whispered into her ear. She was hovering next to Kate. "Think, but don't think. Hold the idea lightly in your mind. Feel the air lift you."

Kate tried to think and *not* think about flying. She felt the night air on her bare arms. She pushed against it and rose up . . . up. . . .

In an instant, Kate was higher than the Home Tree. She swooped through the air. Cool air rushed against her face. She was flying!

How could this have ever been hard? she wondered. It seemed so easy now.

Kate found that she could use her arms like rudders to turn. She dipped down and felt leaves brush against her toes. She shot up through the air again and made a loop.

"You've got it, child! Now try going

faster!" Vidia sped ahead. Kate chased after her.

"Faster!" Vidia shrieked. Kate sped up again. She was flying faster than she'd ever thought she could.

But Vidia flew faster still, so fast she looked like a shooting star in the night. Kate could hear her tiny voice crying, "Faster! Faster!"

Kate laughed with joy. Below her, Never Land lay spread out like a patchwork quilt. Light patches of sand and rock were mixed with darker patches of trees. Above, stars glittered coldly in the velvet black sky.

"Where should we go?" she shouted to Vidia.

"Anywhere!" came the faint reply.

In the distance, Kate saw a tall mountain. She aimed herself toward it.

Suddenly, a large shape burst out at her. Two yellow eyes flashed in the darkness. Kate screamed and threw her hands in front of her face. She dropped in the air, just missing the owl.

The bird screeched its annoyance at her, then flapped away.

Kate regained her balance. "That was a close one," she said in a shaky voice. She was trembling all over. "Can we stop for a minute? Vidia?"

There was no answer. She scanned the sky, but she didn't see Vidia's glow.

Kate looked down. Her belt loop was empty. Vidia was gone—and so was the rest of the fairy dust.

Chapter 9

Tink sat on the bench in her workshop. Sunlight gleamed off the saucepan as she studied the crack in its handle. "A tricky fix," she murmured. "Very tricky—"

"Tink!" a voice interrupted.

"Not now," Tink told it. "I'm busy."

"Tink!" the voice insisted. "Wake up!"

Tink opened her eyes. She wasn't in her workshop. She was in a hammock in the willow room. Mia and Gabby were staring down at her.

Tink frowned at them. "I was having the nicest dream," she said.

"Prilla told us to wake you," Mia said. "Kate's gone."

Tink sat up and yawned. "Maybe she went for a walk."

Mia shook her head. "We asked around. Nobody in Pixie Hollow has seen her."

Never a moment's peace with these Clumsies, Tink thought with a sigh. *But at least it will be over soon.* Today the girls would return to their own homes, and Tink could go back to her workshop. Just the thought of it filled her with energy. She hopped out of bed. "All right. Let's find her," she said.

Outside, they met up with Prilla and Lainey. "We just came from the beach," said Prilla. "We didn't see Kate there, either."

"Well, it's still early," Tink said. "She can't have gone very far."

Just then, they saw Terence coming toward them. Right away, Tink knew something was wrong. Terence's wings sagged, and his glow was dim.

"What's the matter?" Tink asked, concerned.

"Someone stole some fairy dust from the mill," Terence said.

"Vidia!" Prilla said with a gasp. "But how did she get it?" Vidia had stolen dust before, more than once. Because of this, she could no longer go near the mill. The queen had used fairy magic to make sure of it.

But Terence shook his head. "It wasn't

Vidia. Not this time. You'd better come see this." He glanced at Mia, Lainey, and Gabby, adding, "You come, too."

They followed Terence downstream to the mill. A pumpkin-canister was sitting outside its doors. Terence lifted the lid. "This was full yesterday."

Tink and Prilla looked inside. Only a thin dusting—not even a cupful—remained in the bottom.

"A Clumsy stole the rest," Terence said, looking hard at the girls.

"You think *we* stole it?" Lainey squeaked, stunned.

"We didn't steal anything!" Mia said. Her dark eyes flashed. She put her arm around Gabby protectively.

"Then explain this," said Terence. He pointed to the mill door. There, outlined

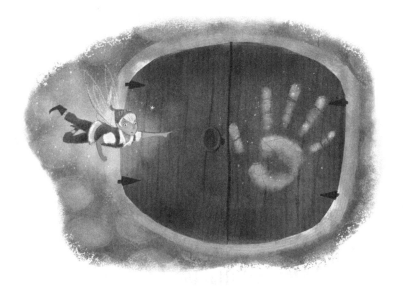

in fairy dust, was a girl-sized handprint.

The girls looked at each other with round eyes. "You don't suppose . . . ?" Lainey began.

"Kate wouldn't steal," Mia said. But she didn't sound certain.

"Kate's missing," Tink explained to Terence. "Since last night."

"If she took the fairy dust, she could be on the other side of Never Land by now," he said. "It could take days to find her."

"Today's the day the girls are supposed to go home!" Prilla said. She turned to Tink. "What should we do?"

Tink tugged on her bangs. She thought of the saucepan waiting in her workshop. Then she looked around at the girls' worried faces. She imagined Kate, lost in Never Land. Suddenly, the saucepan didn't seem so important.

"Gather up all the fairies you can find," Tink told Prilla. "Kate's somewhere out there." She swept an arm toward the forest. "It may take all of Pixie Hollow to find her."

*

Prilla hurried to tell the messenger-talent fairies about Kate. The messengers alerted the scouts. Within minutes, the scouts had fanned out across the forest, searching for a sign of the lost girl.

The water-talent fairies joined the search, too. They paddled their leaf-boats along Havendish Stream, calling Kate's name up and down the banks.

Meanwhile, animal-talent fairies took to the skies. They rode on the backs of blue jays and starlings. They circled high in the air, hoping to catch a glimpse of Kate.

Prilla waited at the Home Tree with Mia, Lainey, and Gabby. Tink hadn't wanted them to join the search. "You can't get far walking," she'd said. "And it's too easy to get lost in the forest if you don't know the way."

"I want to fly and look for Kate, too," Gabby said as they watched the fairies fly high above them.

"We can't," Mia told her. "There isn't any extra fairy dust for us to fly with. Kate took it."

Gabby stuck out her lower lip. "That's not fair."

"No, it isn't," Mia agreed with a frown.

"Anyway," Gabby said, "I don't need fairy dust to fly. I can use my wings."

"Mia, you don't think Kate left us on purpose, do you?" Lainey asked.

"I don't know," Mia said, her frown deepening. It was clear she'd been thinking the same thing.

Lainey squinted up at the sun. It was high in the sky now. The day was passing quickly. "What will we do if we can't find

Kate before we have to leave?" she asked.

Nobody answered. No one knew. "We'll find her," Prilla said at last, trying to sound confident. "All of Pixie Hollow is out looking for her now."

"Where's Gabby?" Lainey said suddenly.

"What do you mean?" asked Mia. "She was right here a second ago."

The girls and Prilla looked all around the Home Tree. Then they looked around the trees nearby. Lainey even ran back to the willow room to check. There was no sign of Gabby.

"I should have been watching her," Mia said. "Where could she be?"

"She said she wanted to fly," Lainey remembered. "You don't think she went looking for Kate, do you?"

"She can't fly," Prilla said. "She doesn't have any fairy dust."

"But she *believes* she can fly," Mia said.

They all turned toward the forest. "Oh, no," Prilla said. "Now we have *two* lost girls."

*

Tink and her friend Beck, an animal-talent fairy, were sweeping over the forest on the back of a starling. It was their third pass that morning. But they still hadn't spotted Kate.

"Do you think she could have gotten as far as Torth Mountain?" Beck shouted over the rushing wind.

Tink stared at the tall mountain in the distance. It was hard to say how far away it was, or whether Kate might have reached

it. Never Land was always changing in size. That was part of the island's magic. Sometimes it might take days to cross it. Other times it might take only hours.

"I guess we could have a look," Tink said with a last glance at the forest.

Just then, something shiny on the ground caught Tink's eye. She looked closer. At first she thought it was a giant dragonfly. Then she realized it was Gabby's shiny wings.

How in the name of Never Land did she get all the way out here? Tink wondered.

Tink didn't know it, but Never Land was exactly how Gabby had gotten there. The island had felt Gabby's belief. It had shrunk itself to help the little girl.

Gabby looked up and spotted the

fairies. She waved her hands and shouted something.

Tink and Beck swooped closer on their bird. Finally, they heard what Gabby was shouting.

"I found Kate! I did! I found her!" Gabby pointed to a nearby tree.

And there, Tink saw, was Kate, tangled high up among its branches.

chapter 10

Once Kate had been found, Tink and Beck
sent a call out to the rest of the fairies.
Everyone, including Mia and Lainey,
hurried to the big oak tree. They could all
see Kate high in the branches. She looked
tired and scared.

Of course, the next problem was how
to get her down. Luckily, this was just
the sort of problem Tink enjoyed solving.
After much tinkering, she rigged up a
pulley system. She made the pulley herself,

using old mouse-cart wheels. The harvest fairies attached it to the highest branches. Then everyone helped to hoist Kate down.

On the ground, Kate hugged her friends. When she heard that Gabby was the one who'd found her, she gave the little girl an extra hug. Kate told them about her flying lesson with Vidia and how she'd ended up in the tree.

"When I couldn't find Vidia, I got scared. I tried to land, but it was dark. I couldn't see where I was going, and I crashed into the oak tree," she explained. "I couldn't fly anymore, either. I guess I'd used up my fairy dust."

"Why didn't you use the dust you took from the mill?" Terence asked.

"It's gone," Kate said. "I had it tied to my belt loop, but now it's missing."

"Vidia took it, I bet," Tink said.

"So that's what Vidia was up to," Prilla said with a frown. "She got Kate to steal dust from the mill so she could have it all for herself."

Kate was shocked. "I didn't steal! Vidia said . . ."

Kate trailed off. From the looks on her friends' faces, she knew that Vidia hadn't told her the truth. "I wouldn't have taken it if I had known it was stealing," she said. "I just wanted to learn how to fly. I thought if we all knew how to fly, we could find our way back to Pixie Hollow."

"You wanted to come back?" Prilla asked.

"More than anything," Kate said. The other girls nodded. "But now I've gone and messed it all up, haven't I?"

To her surprise, Tink flew over and landed on her shoulder. To Kate, it felt as if a butterfly were resting there. "You haven't messed anything up," Tink said. "And you might find your way back here still. I would be glad to see you."

"Oh!" Prilla said then. "Look how late it's getting! If we don't go now, we may miss our chance to get you to the mainland!"

The sun was low in the sky. It was time for the girls to go to the fairy circle—and then home.

*

Before they could leave, though, they had to say good-bye to Queen Clarion. They found her waiting for them at the fairy circle. She was perched on the snow-white toadstool, looking as queenly as ever.

One by one, the girls said their good-byes. Kate stepped forward last.

"I'm sorry I lost all your fairy dust," she said to the queen.

"We'll get it back—most of it, anyway,"

Queen Clarion replied. "Vidia will return eventually. Pixie Hollow is her home. No Never fairy can stay away for long."

That made Kate feel a little better. There were many other things she wanted to say about how much she loved Pixie Hollow and Havendish Stream and the orchard and the willow room and all the fairies she'd met. Instead, she said, "Thanks for being so nice to us."

The queen smiled and said, "You are always welcome in Pixie Hollow." She held out her tiny hand. Ever so gently, Kate grasped it between her thumb and forefinger and shook it.

Kate stepped into the center of the fairy circle, where her friends and Prilla were waiting. Rain was there with her funny little pinwheel. "The tide is

forwarding. Mark is aflay," she said.

"She means," said Skye, "it's time to go."

The girls joined hands. Prilla landed on Gabby's upturned palm. They were all together, just as they had been when they arrived in Never Land.

"Bye-bye, fairies!" Gabby shouted.

The other girls joined her. "Good-bye! Good-bye!" they called.

"Fly safely!" The queen and Terence waved. Tink just reached for her bangs. Not because she was annoyed this time, but because she wanted to hide her misty eyes.

Then Prilla blinked, and the world blinked, too.

But when the girls opened their eyes, nothing had changed. They were still standing in the fairy circle.

"It didn't work," Kate murmured.

"What?" Rain frowned and shook her pinwheel. Then she said a lot of jingly things the girls couldn't understand.

"She means," said Skye, looking embarrassed, "that we may have made an error or two."

But the girls were all smiling. "It didn't work," Kate said again, more loudly. "We don't have to go home! Not just yet."

The girls stood hand in hand. Tink fluttered over and landed on Kate's shoulder. Together, they watched the sun sink below the horizon.

Not one of them doubted that they would make it home someday. But in the meantime, they had many adventures ahead of them in Never Land.

Lainey couldn't shake the idea
that the flamingo was trying
to tell her something.

The Never Girls

the
space
between

Written by
Kiki Thorpe

Illustrated by
Jana Christy

A STEPPING STONE BOOK™

RANDOM HOUSE 🏠 NEW YORK

Chapter 1

Lainey Winters was soaring.

For a brief moment, her heart seemed to stop. The ground fell away, and she rose up, up, up . . . and over the fallen log.

An instant later, she touched down again, bounding through the forest on the back of a doe. Trees flashed by in a blur of green. Lainey dug her hands deeper into the doe's fur. She held on tight as they darted around bushes and flew over stones.

Leaves crashed above. Lainey looked up and saw a squirrel racing through the trees. A tiny fairy sat on its back, her long brown braid swinging behind her. The squirrel leaped from branch to branch, keeping pace with the doe.

Lainey leaned forward, urging her doe on. The fairy did the same.

Ahead was a small clearing. In its center stood a tall maple tree, bigger than any other tree in the forest. From a distance, its branches seemed to sparkle and move. This was due to the many fairies who hummed around it like bees around a honeycomb. The maple was called the Home Tree, and it was the heart of Pixie Hollow, the Never fairies' world.

Lainey steered the doe toward the Home Tree. Even without looking up,

she could sense the fairy on the squirrel following above.

A few feet from the tree, the squirrel shot past Lainey. It landed on a branch and came to a stop just as Lainey and the doe pulled up at the Home Tree's roots.

Lainey laughed. "You beat me again, Fawn!" she called to the fairy on the squirrel.

"I wouldn't be much of an animal-talent fairy if I couldn't win a race against a Clumsy, would I?" Fawn replied, smiling.

Lainey slid off the doe's back, pushing the big glasses she wore up her nose. She didn't care about winning or losing. For her, the joy was in riding the deer, feeling it turn when she wanted to turn, knowing when it would leap. In her real life, the one where she went to school and lived with her parents, Lainey had never even had a pet, not so much as a goldfish. But here in Never Land, she'd played hide-and-seek with wild hares. She'd listened to the songs of loons. She'd cradled baby hedgehogs in her hand. Things she'd never dreamed possible seemed to happen every day.

As Lainey patted the deer's back, Fawn flew down and landed on its head. She whispered something in the doe's ear. The doe ducked its head once, as if nodding. Then it turned and bounded away into the forest.

"What did you say?" Lainey asked.

"I told her next time I'd ride with her, and you could ride the squirrel," Fawn joked.

"I want to learn to do that," Lainey said.

Fawn raised her eyebrows. "Ride a squirrel? Don't you think you're a bit too big?"

Lainey giggled. "No, I want to learn how to speak Deer."

"You have to wriggle before you can hop," Fawn replied.

"I have to do what?" asked Lainey, confused.

"It's an animal-fairy saying," Fawn explained. "It means you have to start slowly. Talking to deer is tricky. They can be pretty snooty about accents. Let's hear how your Mouse is coming along."

Furrowing her brow, Lainey squeaked, *"Eeee-eee!"*

Fawn had been teaching Lainey how to speak the language of mice. So far, Lainey had only learned one squeak. Loosely translated, it meant "Are your whiskers well?"

Two dairy mice that were sniffing around nearby lifted their heads to look at Lainey.

"Not bad," said Fawn, nodding. "Now let's hear you call that chickadee." She pointed to a plump little bird sitting on a branch.

"But I don't know Chickadee!" Lainey protested.

"It's easy," said Fawn. "Just go like this." Pursing her lips, Fawn let out a whistle that sounded like *tseedle dee tseedle dee deet.* "You try."

Lainey did her best to copy Fawn.

She pursed her lips and whistled. But all that came out was a sad *feewp*!

To her surprise, the chickadee flew over and landed on her finger.

"How did I do that?" Lainey asked. Then she noticed Fawn laughing. "Wait a second. *You* called him over, didn't you?"

"So what if I did?" Fawn said with an impish grin. "He wouldn't have come if he didn't want to. Animals like you, Lainey. I'd say you're becoming a real animal-talent Clumsy."

Lainey blushed.

Fawn pulled a sunflower seed from her pocket. She held it out to the chickadee, who took it in his beak and flew away.

"Well, I'm hungry," Fawn said. "Want to see what the baking-talent fairies have whipped up today?"

Lainey shook her head. "I'm going to go find the other girls. See you later?"

"Sure," said Fawn. "I think there's a nest of robin's eggs that need a hand with hatching. Maybe you can help me." With a wave, she flew off.

Lainey started across the meadow, her spirits high. Fawn's compliment still rang in her ears. *A real animal-talent Clumsy.* Lainey couldn't help smiling every time she thought about it.

Maybe it's true, Lainey thought. *Maybe I really do have animal talent.*

Before coming to Pixie Hollow, Lainey had never felt particularly special. She wasn't beautiful like her friend Mia, or brave like her friend Kate. She wasn't good at sports, and she didn't get the best grades in school. In fact, Lainey hadn't been sure she was good at anything at all.

But that had changed when she'd started spending time with the animal-talent fairies. Lainey was learning how to listen to animals and how to watch them. And she had a knack for it!

A real animal-talent Clumsy.

A rustling noise above her made Lainey look up. She paused to watch a flock of flamingos pass. She loved seeing the pale pink birds against the brilliant blue of the sky. The flamingos had been one of the very first creatures she'd seen in Never Land, and she never tired of watching them.

Lainey continued across the meadow and made her way to Havendish Stream. There she found Kate, Mia, and Gabby, her friends who had come to Never Land with her. They were sailing boats with the water-talent fairies. Tiny fairies in red, gold, and green leaf-boats drifted around on the current while the girls blew wind into their sails.

The freckled, curly-haired fairy named Prilla was there, too. Prilla was the reason the girls had come to Never Land. She

had a talent unlike any other in Pixie Hollow. She could travel to the world of humans and back again just by blinking. One day, she'd traveled to Mia and Gabby's backyard and accidentally brought the four girls back to Pixie Hollow with her.

Prilla had discovered that she couldn't blink the girls back home, so the fairies of Pixie Hollow had taken them in. That had been days ago—or was it weeks? Lainey wasn't sure. Time passed strangely in Never Land, where every day was sunny and no one ever grew up or grew old.

"Hi, Lainey," Mia said. "Where have you been?"

"I was riding in the woods with Fawn," Lainey said.

Kate stood, brushing off the knees of her jeans. "We're thinking about going to

Skull Rock, just to see what it's like," she told Lainey. Kate had made it her mission to explore every corner of Never Land.

"Prilla says we might see a mermaid there!" Gabby chimed in excitedly. Gabby was only five, but she was every bit as adventurous as the other girls.

"We're not going for long," Mia added. "There's a fairy dance tonight, and I want to make sure we're back in time. The weaving-talent fairies are going to braid jasmine into my hair!"

"Want to come?" Kate asked Lainey.

Lainey hesitated. She wanted to go with her friends, but she also wanted to watch chicks hatching with Fawn. There were so many fun things happening in Never Land. Sometimes it was hard to decide what to do first.

Just then, they spotted a fairy flying toward them. As she came closer, the girls saw it was Skye. The fairy's rose-petal cap was crooked on her head, and she seemed to be out of breath.

"I've been looking all over for you girls!" she said with a gasp. "It's time!"

"Time for what?" asked Kate.

"Never Land is on the move again," Skye replied.

The girls looked at each other in dismay. They knew what that meant. It was time for them to go home.

Chapter 2

Skye, the seeing-talent fairy, was the one who had figured out how the girls had come to Never Land. She'd also figured out why they couldn't return home again.

As Skye had explained it, Never Land was unlike other islands. It drifted on the seas of children's dreams, moving wherever it wished. One day, it had drifted close to the world of Clumsies, so close that the tiniest bit of magic had pulled four unsuspecting girls to its shores. Kate, Mia, Lainey, and Gabby had always believed in fairies, but their wildest dreams came true when they arrived there on Prilla's blink.

Then the island had drifted away again—and the four girls had been stranded.

But now Never Land was close to the girls' world again. "I saw the mainland with my own eyes," Skye told the girls. "Prilla can blink you back home again— right away! But you must hurry!"

"But what about Skull Rock?" said Kate.

"And the mermaid?" said Gabby.

"And the fairy dance?" said Mia.

"And the robin chicks?" said Lainey.

"If you don't go now, you might never make it back. Who knows when Never

Land will be this close to your world again?" Skye said.

The girls had always known this day would come. They just hadn't thought it would come so soon. Not one of them wanted to leave, but if they didn't, they might never see their families again.

So they would have to say good-bye— to the flower-filled meadow and burbling Havendish Stream, to the magnificent Home Tree and all the kind, lovely fairies who lived there. *And it isn't just a "see-you-later" good-bye,* Lainey thought. *It is really and truly farewell.* Children who left Never Land never came back, the fairy Tinker Bell had told them. They grew up too quickly and forgot about it.

With heavy hearts, the four girls went to their willow-tree room to pack.

Sunlight shone through the willow's branches as they entered, casting a jade-green glow over the room. Lainey looked at the hammocks where they'd slept, the firefly lanterns hanging from the tree limbs, the moss carpet on the ground.

"There isn't anything to pack," she realized. They'd come to Pixie Hollow with nothing but the clothes they had on.

"I want to take *something* home with me," Mia said. She picked up a tiny folding fan that a fairy had left behind. The fan was made from daisy petals held together with pine needles. Mia put it in her pocket.

Kate found an itty-bitty kaleidoscope that a pots-and-pans fairy had cobbled together from bits of scrap metal. A water-talent fairy had cast the lens from a single drop of dew. Gabby chose a daisy garland

that the garden-talent fairies had woven.
She placed it on her head like a crown.

"It'll wilt, you know," Mia warned her
little sister.

"I don't care," Gabby said, sticking out her lip.

Lainey looked around for a souvenir of her own. She considered her licorice-twig toothbrush or one of the firefly lanterns, but neither seemed right. She wished she could take a pet home with her—her doe, maybe, or one of the livelier squirrels. But of course, she knew the animals belonged in Never Land. Besides, her mother would never allow it—her mother didn't even like goldfish.

At last she picked up a mouse-herder's lasso. It was made of braided Never grass. Lainey slipped it over her wrist like a bracelet, pulling the end tight. She remembered the day Fawn had used it to lasso a wayward dairy mouse.

Thinking of that reminded Lainey of

her lesson earlier that day. *I'll never learn how to speak Deer now.* The thought filled Lainey with sadness.

Prilla appeared in the doorway of the willow room. Her bright, open face was unusually glum. "Skye says you must hurry. There isn't much time."

Taking one last look around their room, the girls followed Prilla out the door.

Beneath a hawthorn tree on the far side of Pixie Hollow was a ring of mushrooms. This was the fairy circle, where Pixie Hollow's magic was strongest. When Lainey and her friends got there, they were surprised to see all the fairies gathered together. Animal fairies, fast-flying fairies, water fairies, light fairies, garden fairies, harvest fairies, baking fairies, dressmaking fairies, art fairies, storytelling fairies, and dozens more. Fairies from every talent had come to see the girls off.

Clarion, queen of the Never fairies, stood at the head of the fairy circle. Her wings were folded solemnly behind her in honor of the sad moment. She nodded to the girls to step inside the circle.

"The fairies have a parting gift for you," the queen said. At her cue, Terence, a dust-talent sparrow man, flew forward. He held out a velvet sack no bigger than a peach pit.

"It's a bit of fairy dust," the queen explained. "Just one pinch for each of you. Perhaps one day you can use it to find your way back to Pixie Hollow."

"How will we know the way?" Kate wondered. "Is there a map?"

The queen spread her hands. "I can't say for sure. Never Land drifts about on the waves, always moving. But some say that to get here from the mainland you should look for the Second Star to the Right and fly straight on till morning."

Thanking the queen, Kate took the bag of dust from Terence and put it in her pocket.

Several fairies and sparrow men came forward then to say special good-byes to the girls. Lainey searched the crowd for Fawn, but she didn't see her friend anywhere.

At last, Skye entered the circle. "You must go now," she told Prilla and the girls. "Never Land is on the move again. Soon it will be too late."

Kate, Lainey, Mia, and Gabby held

hands. Prilla landed in Gabby's open palm.

"Fly sa—" the queen started to say as Prilla blinked.

In that moment, all of Pixie Hollow winked out. The trees, the flowers, the sky, the fairy circle, and the fairies themselves—everything vanished. The rest of Queen Clarion's words were lost.

*

An instant later, the girls found themselves in Mia and Gabby's backyard. They looked around at the tall wooden fence, the neatly mowed lawn, and the tidy rows of petunias in the flower bed.

A soccer ball sat nearby in the grass. Lainey picked it up, turning it over in her hands. They'd been playing a game with the ball just before they blinked to Never

Land. That seemed like a lifetime ago. Like something she'd dreamed.

"Are we really home?" asked Gabby.

Kate pinched herself. "I think so," she said, but she didn't sound certain.

They heard a high bell-like noise, like the tinkle of a fairy's laugh. All the girls turned toward the sound, but it was only Mia's cat, Bingo. The bells on Bingo's collar jingled as he ran toward them.

Mia scooped the cat up in her arms. She buried her face in his fur. "Oh, Bingo! I missed you!"

"*Mrow,*" Bingo complained as Mia squeezed him tightly. He wriggled out of her arms and wandered off to chase grasshoppers.

Just then, the back door to the house opened. "Gabby, are you out here?" called a familiar voice.

"Mami!" Gabby squealed. She went running toward her mother, her curls bouncing and her fairy wings flapping on her back.

Mia turned to Lainey and Kate with wide eyes. "What am I going to tell her?" she whispered. "We've been gone for *days!*"

"Remember what Prilla taught us about a blink," Lainey reminded her. "When she travels on a blink, time moves differently."

"Let's hope it's true." Kate looked worried. "Otherwise, we're all going to be in for it."

"Do you think it's the same if we fly to Never Land?" Lainey wondered. "Does time stop the same way?"

"Speaking of that," Mia said, "what about the fairy dust? Shouldn't we put it somewhere safe?"

"It's plenty safe. I've got it right here," Kate said, patting her pocket.

An odd look flashed across her face. Kate dug her hand into her pocket. Then she checked her other pocket. She turned both pockets inside out.

Mia frowned. "Kate, that's not funny. Quit messing around."

"I'm not joking," Kate said in a choked voice. "The fairy dust—it's gone!"

Chapter 3

Fawn sat alone in the Home Tree courtyard, twirling the end of her braid between her fingers. Lainey, Mia, Kate, and Gabby had gone to the fairy circle— any moment now, they'd be on their way back to their real homes. Fawn knew she should see them off. But she couldn't bring herself to go.

Fawn hated good-byes. As a Never fairy, she rarely had to say them. Fairies hardly ever left Pixie Hollow, and when they did it was never for long. As for her animal friends, Fawn could see them whenever she wanted, because the creatures of Never Land never grew old.

But now her new Clumsy friends were gone, and she hadn't said so much as "fly safely." Not even to Lainey, whom Fawn liked especially. Fawn felt tears pricking at the backs of her eyes.

"You knew this day would come," she scolded herself. "There's no sense crying over it."

At last, Fawn got to her feet. But instead of flying to the fairy circle, she flew in the opposite direction, toward the dairy barn. When Fawn's spirits were low, she liked to visit the dairy mice. She was always happiest around animals.

As Fawn pulled open the heavy door,

the mice lifted their heads in greeting.

"How are you, Thistledown? Feeling well, Cloverseed?" she asked as she walked among them. The mice came forward to snuffle her pockets, the bells around their necks chiming faintly. Fawn scratched them behind their ears.

"Where's Milkweed?" she wondered, noticing an empty stall.

The mice only blinked in reply. Fawn understood mice well enough to know that not one of them had noticed Milkweed was missing until now. Mice could be self-centered that way.

"I reckon he's wandered off," she said. "Probably raiding Rosetta's garden for seeds again." Milkweed was a good name for the missing mouse because, like a weed, he was always turning up where he wasn't wanted. "I'll have to go find him."

Fawn was glad to have something to do to take her mind off the girls. Leaving the dairy barn, she headed outside, calling for Milkweed in soft squeaks. "Milkweed! Where are you, you little fur ball?"

Fawn looked in Rosetta's garden, but she didn't see Milkweed there. She tried other gardens, then circled Pixie Hollow, flying in wider and wider loops.

When she came to Havendish Stream, she paused. Beyond was the great forest of Never Land. Fawn didn't think the little mouse could have crossed the stream on his own.

She was about to turn back when her eyes fell on the stream bank. There in the mud, clear as day, was a mouse's footprint.

Fawn sighed. "Oh, bugs and beetles.

What are you up to now, Milkweed?"

She flew across the stream and came to a stop in front of a massive fig tree. It was so large that it looked like several trees grown together. At the base of the tree was a hollow she had never noticed before. To Fawn, the hole seemed as big as a cave.

Were Fawn's ears playing tricks on her or did she hear a bell? She listened carefully. Yes, there it was—a faint jingling. It seemed to be coming from inside the fig tree.

She peered cautiously into the hollow. Fawn wasn't afraid of most animals. She'd talked her way out of tight spots with snakes, badgers, even an owl. Still, she wasn't foolish enough to walk blindly into a predator's nest.

"Helloooooo?" Fawn called into the darkness. Silence greeted her.

Taking a deep breath, Fawn flew into the tree.

Like all fairies, Fawn glowed. But her glow only allowed her to see a couple of inches in front of her. She flew slowly, shivering as she brushed against cobwebs.

Fawn could no longer hear the bell. "Milkweed?" she called.

Just then, Fawn saw light ahead. But how could that be? Wasn't the mouth of the hollow behind her? Had she gotten turned around? *Fawn, you doodlehead,* she said to herself. *You've been flying in a circle!*

If Milkweed had ever been inside the hollow tree, he wasn't anymore, Fawn decided. She headed toward the opening.

Sunshine flooded her eyes. Fawn stopped, blinking in surprise at the strange landscape before her.

A sea of green grass stretched below her feet. But what odd grass! Every blade had been snipped off at the exact same height. Fawn flew down close to examine the grass, trying to imagine what creature could have cut it just so. *Why,* she thought, *even the most talented harvest fairies couldn't have been so precise!*

And the flowers! Fawn stared in amazement. They grew in tidy rows, lined up as neatly as marching ants. Flowers in Pixie Hollow grew hither and thither, wherever the wind—or the garden fairies—planted them.

"What is this place?" Fawn murmured.

Then Fawn saw something that made her catch her breath. Ahead, a massive structure rose up from the grass, so high it seemed to touch the sky. Fawn could tell from the doors and windows that the thing was a house. But who would live in such a house? It was bigger than the entire Home Tree! Big enough to hold a whole *family* of Clumsies . . .

With a start, Fawn realized that she was looking at a Clumsy house. "But that's impossible!" she said aloud. Clumsies lived on the mainland, a place far, far from Pixie Hollow. So what was a Clumsy house doing inside an old fig tree?

Fawn knew she should fly straight back to the Home Tree and tell the queen what she'd found. But her curiosity got the better of her. Instead of going back, Fawn flew forward.

Right away, Fawn could tell she was no longer in Pixie Hollow. The air felt different. It *smelled* different. She could hear birds singing, but she didn't recognize their songs. Fawn heard other noises, too—strange rumbling sounds that came and went like ocean waves. For the life of her, she couldn't have said what made them.

Fawn flew slowly through the flowers, enjoying the sense of adventure. *What kinds of animals live here?* she wondered. In Fawn's opinion, you couldn't know much about a place until you met its animals.

The house loomed in front of her. Flying up to a window, Fawn peeked inside. She saw what looked like a sitting room. There were chairs, lamps, and a table. Books and shoes were scattered everywhere. But she didn't see any Clumsies.

Somewhere nearby, a bell jingled faintly.

"Milkweed?" Fawn called. She looked behind her, but the mouse didn't show a whisker.

There's something funny about that jingle, Fawn thought with a frown. Whatever was wearing the bell didn't move like a mouse.

Fawn spun around just in time to see something lunge toward her. She screamed. As she leaped from the windowsill, she caught a glimpse of yellow eyes and needle-sharp teeth.

Fawn zigzagged back the way she'd

come, searching for the hollow fig tree. But each way she turned, she saw only a tall wooden fence. "Where is it?" she wailed, lurching this way and that. *"Where is it?"*

With a cold jolt of fear, Fawn realized that the tree wasn't there. The passage back to Pixie Hollow was gone!

Fawn glanced back over her shoulder. She saw now that her pursuer was a cat. His brown fur was striped like a tiger's, and his eyes were like bits of amber. They narrowed as he stalked toward Fawn, his tail twitching eagerly.

Fawn gave up looking for the fig tree and searched for any escape. Along one side of the fence, she noticed a narrow gap between the wooden slats. It would be a tight squeeze. But it was her only chance.

Fawn raced toward the gap in the

fence. She reached it just as the cat leaped. Fawn wriggled and twisted, trying to squeeze her wings through. She felt one of the boards move slightly, as though it was loose, and at last she shot through the gap. Behind her, the cat slammed against the fence with an angry yowl.

Fawn looked up and gasped. She was back in Pixie Hollow!

"Wh-what ... how ... ?" Fawn stuttered. She spun around. She was hovering in front of the hollow fig tree.

Fawn's wings felt like they were going to give out. She sank to the ground, trembling all over. *It doesn't matter how I got here,* she thought. *The important thing is that I'm still alive.*

Fawn glanced back at the hollow tree and shivered. The tree was dangerous. She knew she had better tell Queen Clarion about it right away.

As Fawn got up to leave, she heard a faint jingle. She looked back at the hollow. Two yellow eyes peered at her from the darkness.

"Oh no!" Fawn cried as a blur of brown fur streaked toward her. She'd led the cat right into Pixie Hollow!

chapter 4

Lainey trudged down the sidewalk in a haze of disappointment. She, Kate, Gabby, and Mia had searched all over Mia's backyard for the lost bag of fairy dust. They'd combed the flower bed, peeked under the patio furniture, and crawled on their knees over the grass. They would have gone on searching, too, if Mia's mother hadn't said it was getting late and sent them home.

Lainey's house was just three doors down from Mia's, along a street lined with tall, narrow homes and spindly trees. Lainey was so used to the path that she hardly noticed where her feet were taking her.

A ferocious bark startled her out of her thoughts. Lainey jumped back as a black-and-white dog threw itself against the fence she was passing.

Lainey saw this dog every time she walked to Mia's house. Although Lainey loved all animals, she'd been careful to steer clear of this one. The dog was always barking.

But maybe now she didn't need to be afraid. After all, she'd learned so much from Fawn. She'd befriended all kinds of animals in Never Land. Maybe she could make friends with this dog, too. *Someone with real animal talent could,* Lainey thought.

And hadn't Fawn told her she had animal talent?

Lainey took a step toward the fence. "There, there," she said soothingly. She didn't know how to speak Dog. But she mimicked the tone Fawn used when she was talking to an upset animal. "Don't be so grouchy. I'm your friend."

The dog paused mid-bark. It stood with its nose against the fence, watching her. "Good dog," Lainey said.

At once the dog began to bark again, louder than ever. Lainey turned and ran the rest of the way to her house.

As soon as she saw her front door, a wave of homesickness washed over her. Lainey took the steps two at a time and burst through the front door, crying, "I'm back! I'm back!"

"I'm in here, Lainey!" her mother called.

Lainey followed the sound of her voice to the kitchen. Her mother was standing with her back to the door, staring up at the open cupboard.

Tears sprang to Lainey's eyes. How long had it been since she'd seen her mother? Days? *Weeks?* Only now did Lainey realize how much she'd missed her parents while she was in Never Land. She hurried over to her mom and wrapped her arms around her waist.

"Hi, baby," her mom said distractedly. "How does spaghetti sound for dinner?"

"Spaghetti sounds good." Pushing her glasses up on her nose, Lainey straightened and turned to face her mother. So much had happened to her in Never

Land. Lainey felt different—no, she *was* different. She was sure her mother would see it in her face.

But at that moment, Mrs. Winters was busy searching the cupboard. She moved some cans around, muttering, "I was sure we had tomato sauce. . . ."

Lainey tugged her mother's sleeve. "Mom . . ."

"Yes, Lainey?" her mother asked, without looking down.

"Do you notice anything *different* about me?" asked Lainey.

At last her mother turned. "Oh, honey," she said with a sigh. "When was the last time you combed your hair? You look like you've been living in the jungle!" She ran her fingernails through Lainey's fine blond locks. "Go run a brush through it, then call your dad and ask him to pick up some dinner on the way home from work. It looks like we'll have to have take-out again. We're out of spaghetti sauce."

"Okay," Lainey mumbled, crestfallen. Her throat ached, but this time it wasn't from homesickness. Suddenly, she was painfully aware of everything she'd lost—the doe and the dairy mice and her friendship with Fawn, the fairies and flamingos, the beauty of Never Land and the specialness she'd felt when she was there. Was even that part gone? Now that she was home again, was she just plain old Lainey?

"Goodness, sweetie, don't be upset. We can have spaghetti *tomorrow* night, if you really want," her mother said, misunderstanding.

Lainey sighed heavily and turned to leave. As she did, her gaze fell on something scuttling across the floor. It was a little gray mouse. Lainey stared. She'd never seen a mouse in her house before. A tiny jingling sound seemed to be coming from it. Looking closer, Lainey saw a bell hanging around its neck.

It was one of the fairies' dairy mice!

At that moment, Lainey's mother saw the mouse, too. "Aaah! Get out!" she shrieked, stomping her foot.

"Don't hurt it!" Lainey exclaimed.

But her mother was striding over to the broom closet. She grabbed a broom and began to chase the mouse around the kitchen.

"Mom, stop!" cried Lainey.

"I won't have mice in *my* house!" her mother declared, swiping at it with the broom. The mouse dodged the bristles one last time and disappeared through a crack in the wall.

"You almost killed it!" Lainey wailed.

"Mice are *pests*," her mother said. "They're *vermin* that carry diseases. For all we know, there could be a whole nest of them living behind the walls." She shuddered. "I think I have some mousetraps down in the basement. For heaven's sake, stay away from there," she added as Lainey kneeled down to peek into the crack. "Who knows what kind of germs that thing has."

Her mother stomped off toward the basement. As soon as she was gone, Lainey got down on her hands and knees to look into the hole.

"Eeee-eee," she squeaked softly.

Nothing happened, so she squeaked again. She could see a pair of beady black eyes gleaming inside the hole. "It's okay," Lainey whispered. "I'm your friend."

The mouse wiggled its whiskers, but it wouldn't come closer.

What was going on? Was it possible she'd lost her animal talent when she'd left Never Land?

Then Lainey had a scarier thought. Maybe she'd never had any animal talent after all. Maybe Fawn had only said that to be nice.

Lainey felt worse than ever. But she knew she didn't have time to mope. Her mother would be back with the mousetrap any moment. Lainey had to find a way to keep the mouse safe.

She went to the cupboard and found a plastic container with a lid. Then she took a block of cheese from the refrigerator and cut off a slice.

She put the piece of cheese in front of the mouse hole. Then she stepped back and waited.

A moment passed. Then a pink nose poked out of the hole, followed by a set of whiskers. Slowly, the mouse crept out, sniffing at the cheese.

Slam! Lainey dropped the container over it. Carefully, she slid the plastic lid under the edge, leaving a little opening for air. Now the mouse was trapped.

"I'm sorry, I'm sorry," Lainey whispered to the mouse as she hurried to her room.

She could feel the little animal scrabbling
against the side of the plastic container.
She'd have to find a better place for the
mouse, maybe a shoe box. But still Lainey
felt ashamed. She knew no self-respecting
animal talent would ever trap a mouse

like this. What would Fawn think if she saw Lainey now?

Another, more important question burned in Lainey's mind—what was a mouse from Pixie Hollow doing *here*?

chapter 5

Fawn dodged left, then right, trying to
shake the cat. Her shoulders ached and
her breath came in gasps. She didn't know
how much longer she could keep flying.
But no matter how she twisted and turned,
the cat was always just behind her.

Ahead, Fawn saw a raspberry bush.
She headed straight for it, darting into
the branches with her last bit of strength.

Fawn peered out between the leaves.
She could see the cat watching her hiding

spot with its yellow eyes. "Why are you bothering me?" Fawn called out in Cat. She hadn't talked to many cats before, but the language came to her naturally. Part of an animal-fairy's magic was being able to speak to any creature.

The cat blinked. It was clear that he wasn't used to being questioned by his prey. "Come out where I can see you, shiny bird," he said.

Shiny bird? Fawn thought, confused. Then she understood. *He thinks I'm a bird! He's attracted to my glow.*

"I'm not a bird!" she yelled to the cat. "I'm a fairy!"

The cat blinked again. "Dragonfly?"

Was it possible this cat had never seen a fairy before? "Not a dragonfly. A fairy!" Fawn shouted.

"Flying thing?" the cat said. If he'd had shoulders, he would have shrugged.

Fawn realized she was getting nowhere talking to him. She had to find another way out of this mess.

Fawn plucked a raspberry from the bush. She weighed it in her palm, considering. A single fairy wasn't strong enough to fight a cat. But Fawn knew cats were proud animals. Maybe if she wounded his pride, he would go away.

Fawn threw the berry as hard as she could, hitting the cat squarely between the eyes. The cat jerked back, startled. He tried to shake the berry off his head. Then he lifted his chin and stalked away, as if he had important business elsewhere.

Fawn grinned as the cat broke into a run. Her plan was working!

But a second later, her smile faded. The cat wasn't running *away* from Fawn—he was running *toward* something.

Just beyond the edge of the woods, a mouse cart was passing through the meadow. The cart driver, a sparrow man named Dooley, was whistling to himself. He didn't see the cat creeping up behind him.

"Dooley!" Fawn shrieked. "Look out!"

Too late! The cat landed on the cart, and its load of walnuts spilled across the trail. The cart mice squealed and bolted, throwing Dooley from his seat.

Dooley tried to fly, but the cat caught him between his front paws. He batted him back and forth, toying with him as if he were a ball of yarn.

"Leave him alone, you ratty tabby!" Summoning her courage, Fawn flew right up to the cat's nose and gave his whiskers a yank.

The cat yowled in pain and leaped back. Fawn took the moment to grab

Dooley's hand. She pulled him to safety in a nearby mole hole.

"Are you all right?" Fawn asked. The stunned sparrow man's glow flickered like a firefly. But he didn't have any scratches as far as Fawn could tell.

"Wh-wh—" Dooley stuttered. "Wh-where did that monster *come* from?"

Before Fawn could reply, they heard squeals. Fawn peeked out the hole. The driverless mouse cart was careening in circles as the terrified mice ran this way and that.

"He's going to get the mice!" Fawn cried.

But to her surprise, the cat bounded right past the mouse cart. Something else had caught his eye.

Ahead was the Home Tree, sparkling with the hundreds of fairies who wove in and out of its branches, going about their business.

Fawn gasped. What had she done? In trying to drive the cat away, she'd sent him straight to the heart of the fairies' world!

"Stay here. I'll send someone to help you with the mice," Fawn told Dooley. Then she raced off toward the Home Tree to warn the other fairies.

In the pebbled courtyard in front of the Home Tree's knothole door, a group of fairies sat enjoying a picnic. The cat headed straight toward them, his tail twitching with pleasure.

"Fly!" Fawn screamed. "Fly away!" But she was too far off to be heard.

Wham! The cat pounced, landing in the middle of the picnic. Seashell plates and

acorn teacups crashed to the ground. Cries of horror filled the courtyard. The cat danced on his hind legs, swiping happily at the fairies as they darted out of the way.

In an instant, the Home Tree was in chaos. The singing-talent fairies' songs turned to screams. A laundry-talent fairy dropped a whole line of washing, which sailed away on a breeze. Fairies and sparrow men crashed into each other as they tried to escape.

Fawn grabbed a blueberry from an overturned barrel and threw it at the cat. But the cat was too dazzled by the fairies to even notice. He slinked around the trunk, looking for one to catch.

Between the roots at the back of the Home Tree was the entrance to the kitchen. The doorway was just wide enough to fit a small melon—or a large cat. As Fawn reached the back of the tree, she saw the tip of the cat's fluffy tail disappear inside.

"Oh no!" Fawn gasped. The kitchen fairies would be trapped!

But a second later, the cat came streaking back out. Right behind him came a band of red-faced kitchen fairies. Some hollered and banged on pots and pans. Others pelted the cat with peppercorns.

The cat fled.

"Good thing we were making pepper soup today," the baking-talent fairy Dulcie said when she caught Fawn's eye.

When the cat was a good distance away, he stopped running. He paced back and forth, casting sulky glances at the Home Tree.

"But it looks to me like we haven't seen the last of that cat," Dulcie added.

chapter 6

Lainey awoke to the sound of fairy laughter. *It's Prilla coming to wake us up!* she thought.

She opened her eyes, expecting to see sunlight dappling the branches of the willow-tree room. Instead, she found herself staring at a painted white ceiling.

Lainey sat up. She was in her own bed in her own room. There was no willow tree and no fairy coming to wake her. Only thin sunlight coming through blue curtains and the smell of her parents' coffee brewing—the same things she'd woken to her whole life.

And yet . . . she could still hear a tiny bell-like sound.

Lainey leaned over the side of her bed. There was the old shoe box she'd put on the floor the night before. Holding her breath, Lainey lifted the lid—

The little mouse stood up on his hind legs to greet her, the bell around his neck jingling faintly. Lainey smiled. *So it wasn't a dream after all,* she thought.

"Good morning, fella," she said softly. She held out her finger to the mouse, who sniffed it with interest. He seemed less afraid than he had been the day before.

Now, for the first time, Lainey noticed a notch in his ear. She remembered that one of the dairy mice had a funny ear.

"Milkweed?" she said. "Is that you?"

The mouse didn't seem to hear her. He sniffed around the shoe box, as if looking for a crumb. Lainey was glad to see that he'd eaten the pizza crust she'd left for him the night before.

"I'll bet you're hungry for breakfast," she said. "Coming right up."

Lainey carefully placed the lid back on the box. She pushed it under the bed so her mother wouldn't find it, then went downstairs to get something to eat.

In the kitchen, she found a note from her mother saying she'd gone to pick up a few things at the store and her dad had gone into work. Lainey placed a frozen waffle in the toaster. She had just poured herself a glass of orange juice when the phone rang.

Lainey picked up the phone. It was Mia.

"Mia!" Lainey cried. "Guess what I found—"

"It's awful, Lainey!" Mia interrupted, her voice cracking. "I can't find him anywhere!"

"Can't find who?" asked Lainey, confused.

"Bingo! He's *missing*!" Tearfully, Mia explained that the cat hadn't been seen since the day before. "He didn't come when I called him. I even put out a bowl of tuna fish, but he didn't turn up. He *never* misses tuna fish."

"Maybe he's out exploring," Lainey said.

"He doesn't leave the backyard." Mia sniffled. "I'm worried something bad happened. Will you help me look for him?"

"I'll be right there," Lainey said.

When she'd hung up, Lainey took the waffle out of the toaster. She wrote a quick note to her parents, then hurried upstairs. She fed pieces of waffle to the mouse as she got dressed.

After she was done, Lainey took the mouse out of the shoe box and gently placed him in her sweatshirt pocket. "Don't worry, little fella," she whispered. "I'll take care of you. I promise."

When Lainey got to Mia's house, Mia and Gabby were sitting on the front steps. Mia's eyes were rimmed with red, as if she'd been crying. Kate was there, too, looking as if she hadn't slept very well.

"I was up all night, looking for the Second Star to the Right," Kate told Lainey. "But I couldn't find it. The queen never told us what it was to the right *of*. Not that it matters anyway," she added, "since we lost the fairy dust."

"Guys," said Lainey, "something really weird happened last night. You aren't going to believe it." Reaching into her sweatshirt pocket, she pulled out the little mouse.

Mia jumped back in surprise. "Why are you carrying a mouse around?" she asked Lainey.

"It's not just any mouse," Lainey replied. "It's Milkweed."

"Milkwhat?" asked Kate.

"His name is Milkweed," Lainey explained. "He's one of the fairies' mice."

Gabby stepped forward to pet the mouse. "Hullo, Milkweed," she said, stroking his head with the tip of her finger.

"What's so important about him?" asked Kate.

"Well, that's the thing," said Lainey. "Don't you wonder how he got here?"

"You brought him in your pocket," Kate pointed out.

"But I *found* him in our kitchen last

night," Lainey said. "Don't you think it's strange that a Never Land mouse turned up in my home?"

"Can we talk about this later?" Mia said impatiently. "Right now, we really need to find Bingo!"

The girls decided to split up to look for the cat. Mia and Gabby took one side of the street, while Lainey and Kate took the other. They walked up and down the neighborhood, calling Bingo's name. But they didn't spot so much as a single paw print.

Finally, they returned to Mia and Gabby's house. When Mrs. Vasquez saw how disappointed they looked, she poured them glasses of lemonade. The girls took their drinks into the backyard.

A dark cloud had settled over the group.

"We're never going to find Bingo," Mia said despairingly.

"We're never going to get back to Never Land," added Kate.

Something in the corner of the yard caught Lainey's eye. "Mia," she said, "when did you get that?"

"Get what?" asked Mia.

"That plastic flamingo," Lainey said, pointing to the tall pink bird in the flower bed. At that moment, the flamingo turned its head. It fixed them with a bright yellow eye. *"Awnk!"* it honked.

The girls screamed and jumped to their feet. Lemonade spilled everywhere.

"Mia?" Mrs. Vasquez called from inside the house. "What's going on?"

"Nothing, Mami!" Mia yelled. She looked back at the flamingo. It was perched on one foot in the middle of Mrs. Vasquez's rosebushes. "What is a *flamingo* doing here?" she whispered.

"Maybe it escaped from the zoo?" Kate guessed.

"Maybe," said Lainey, her heart filling with hope, "it came from Never Land!"

The other girls turned to her. But before anyone could reply, they heard footsteps coming from inside the house. "Quick!" Mia whispered. "Hide it!"

"Hide it?" said Kate. "How? It's as tall as we are!"

"I have an idea!" said Lainey. "Kate, kneel down. You too, Mia. Hurry!"

When Mrs. Vasquez stepped outside a moment later, Gabby was sitting on Mia's shoulders. Lainey was sitting on Kate's shoulders. They crowded together in the corner of the yard, blocking the flamingo from her view.

"What on earth are you all doing?" Mrs. Vasquez asked.

"We're having chicken races!" Lainey said brightly as Kate staggered beneath her, trying to keep her balance.

"Awnk!" honked the flamingo behind them.

"Bok!" shouted Lainey. "It's part of the game. You have to say, *'Bok, bok!'"*

"Bok! Bok! Bok!" The girls all began to yell to cover up the noises the flamingo was making.

Mrs. Vasquez frowned. "It looks

dangerous. Can't you girls play something where you all keep your feet on the ground?" She started into the house, then paused and turned back. "And, girls, please don't play too close to the flower bed. Those are my prize roses!" She slid open the screen door and went inside.

"Oof!" Kate grunted as she fell to the grass, tipping Lainey off her shoulders. "You're a lot heavier than you look. Now, what were you saying?"

Lainey's heart was beating fast. "What if the flamingo is from Never Land?" she whispered to her friends.

"What would it be doing here?" asked Mia.

For the first time since they'd lost the fairy dust, Kate's face lit up. "The fairies must have sent him! I'll bet he's here to show us the way back to Never Land!"

At once the girls turned toward the bird. It looked back at them warily.

"Come on, Mr. Bird. Tell us how to get back to Never Land," Kate coaxed.

"Look!" cried Gabby. "He's trying to get away!" The flamingo was spreading his wings, as if he was about to take to the air.

"Not so fast!" cried Kate. She lunged at the flamingo, which hopped just out of her reach. Kate began to chase him through the flower bed. Petals flew from the roses.

"Kate!" Mia wailed. "Watch out for Mami's flowers!"

Kate ignored her and dove into the middle of the petunias. She managed to grab the flamingo by the leg.

"I got him— Ow!" Kate cried as the

flamingo beat her about the head with his wings, trying to escape. "Quick! Someone find something to hold him!"

"I know how to catch him!" Gabby hurried to the back door and grabbed a butterfly net that was leaning up against the house. She ran toward Kate and the flamingo, waving it.

"Don't!" cried Lainey. "He's scared." The flamingo was flapping his wings, straining to get away. At last the bird managed to pull his foot from Kate's grip. He rose into the air, sailed a short distance, and landed on the roof of Mia and Gabby's house.

The girls stared up at him. "Well," said Mia, "*now* what do we do?"

"*Awnk!*" said the flamingo.

chapter 7

Silence had settled across Pixie Hollow. In the gardens, the spider-thread hammocks hung empty. On Havendish Stream, the fairies' leaf-boats bobbed forlornly on their anchors. Not a whisper of wings could be heard across the meadow. The only sound was the splash of the waterwheel as it turned in the stream for an empty mill.

Inside the Home Tree, fairies peeked from the windows. They were watching for the furry beast that had driven them all behind doors. Many fairies had gathered in the grand dining hall. The serving talents were passing out acorn caps full of blackberry tea to soothe everyone's jangled nerves.

As Fawn wandered through the dining hall, she heard snippets of talk among the fairies.

"I've never seen a monster like that in Pixie Hollow before. . . ."

"Did you see it knock down the bridge?"

"We can't stay inside forever! We'll starve, you know. . . ."

In a corner of the dining room, a small group of fairies hovered around Dooley. His glow had returned, but he still wore a tragic look on his face. He clutched a teacup and a plate of poppy-seed cake as he told his story. "I swear on my wings, I

was *inches* from being eaten! My whole life *flashed* before my eyes. Mmm. This is very tasty cake. You know, I think another slice might help me get my strength back. . . ."

Fawn felt terrible. She knew that this was all her fault. If she hadn't flown into the Clumsy garden, the cat never would have chased her into Pixie Hollow.

And yet, Fawn still didn't understand what had happened. How had she gotten to the Clumsy garden to begin with?

Fawn spotted Queen Clarion standing before one of the tall dining hall windows. The queen held a cup of tea in her hand, but she never raised it to her lips. She gazed outside with a puzzled expression. Fawn made her way over to her.

Queen Clarion turned her head. "Oh, Fawn. I was just thinking how strange this all is. Usually Never creatures are respectful of the fairy realm—even the hawks and snakes."

Fawn cleared her throat. "The thing is," she began, "the cat isn't from Never Land."

The queen raised her eyebrows. "Then where did it come from?"

"I, ah, I don't really know," Fawn admitted. Taking a deep breath, she explained how she'd gone looking for Milkweed and instead stumbled upon a Clumsy's house inside an old fig tree.

"What Clumsy?" asked Queen Clarion. "Was it a pirate? Or one of Peter Pan's boys?"

Fawn shook her head. "I don't know. I never saw any Clumsies there. But it wasn't just a house. The grass was different and the flowers were different. It even had a different sky. It was a whole Clumsy world."

"But that's impossible," said the queen. "To get to the world of Clumsies, you'd have to fly across an ocean!"

"I don't understand it, either," said Fawn. "But that's where I saw the cat. He started to chase me. When I tried to escape, I found myself right back in Pixie Hollow—and the cat was with me!"

The queen furrowed her brow. "It doesn't make sense."

Tinker Bell had been sitting nearby, tinkering with a thimble bucket. Suddenly, she spoke up. "Maybe there's a hole."

The queen and Fawn both turned to her. "What do you mean?" asked Queen Clarion.

"Like a shortcut between Never Land and the mainland," said Tink. "Usually, they're far apart. They exist in separate realms. But if there was a hole . . ." Tink took the cup of tea from Queen Clarion's hand and poured it into the bucket. Tea dribbled out the bottom. "Things could fall through."

"If there was a hole, wouldn't we know about it?" asked Queen Clarion.

"It could be a pinprick hole," Tink said. "They're the sneakiest kind. You don't know about them until you spring a leak."

"A hole between Never Land and the mainland," the queen murmured, her frown deepening. "If it's true, all kinds of dangers could reach Pixie Hollow."

Tink nodded. "The cat might be the least of our troubles."

Fawn chewed her lip. She'd just thought of something. "If there's a hole, that means things can go both ways."

"What are you saying?" asked Tink.

"If the cat followed me here, that means he can follow me back." Fawn lifted her chin bravely. "I'll lead the cat back to the Clumsy house. I'll use myself as bait."

The queen looked shocked. "I forbid it," she said. "It's too dangerous."

"It's the only way," Fawn said. "If I don't, we may be stuck inside the Home Tree forever."

Tink stood up. "You can't do it alone. I'll help you."

Fawn was about to say no. But when she saw the fierce look in Tink's eyes, she nodded. She would need all the help she could get.

chapter 8

"Somebody *do* something!" Mia said.

Kate took off her sneaker and hurled it at the flamingo. The shoe sailed through the air, missing the bird by a mile. It landed in the rain gutter.

The flamingo looked at it curiously. It stepped over to the sneaker and began to peck at the laces.

"That's just great," Kate groaned. She threw herself down on the grass. "Now a flamingo is eating my shoe."

"And I still don't know where Bingo is," Mia said, sinking down next to her. "This has got to be the worst day ever."

Lainey and Gabby sat down, too. Lainey took Milkweed from her pocket and stroked his furry head. *I wish I could talk to you,* she thought. *You could tell me what's going on.*

Suddenly, Milkweed twisted in her hands and leaped onto the grass. Before Lainey could grab him, he dashed across the lawn, wriggled through a narrow gap in the fence, and disappeared.

"Oh no!" Lainey jumped up and ran to the fence. She tried to peer between the slats. "Where did he go?"

Gabby put her eye right up to the fence slats. "I see him!" she cried.

"Quick! Kate, Mia, give me a boost!"

Lainey cried. Kate and Mia ran over and lifted Lainey so she could see over the top of the fence. Lainey scanned the neighbor's yard on the other side, but there was no sign of the mouse. "He's gone!"

"But I saw him. I did!" Gabby insisted.

"Well, he's gone now," Lainey said sadly as Mia and Kate helped her down.

Lainey imagined Milkweed loose in the alley. *What if he meets up with a cat or a dog or a mousetrap?* she thought. Even if he escaped those dangers, how would he find food or a safe place to sleep? Their city street was nothing like the mossy hummocks and flower-filled meadows of Pixie Hollow.

Why had he run away like that? All Lainey wanted to do was take care of him, but it seemed she'd failed even in that. She felt a lump in her throat. She couldn't even look after a *mouse*! How disappointed Fawn would be if she knew.

"Look, he's coming back!" Gabby said.

For one hopeful moment, Lainey thought she meant Milkweed. But Gabby was pointing at the house. The girls watched as the flamingo lifted off from the roof. He glided down and landed on the grass a few feet away from Lainey.

"Awnk!" The flamingo turned his head to one side. His beady eye stared at Lainey.

He looks like he wants to tell me something, Lainey thought.

"It's no use," Lainey told the bird bitterly. "I don't understand."

"*Awnk!*" The flamingo took a few steps
toward the fence, then twisted his neck to
look back at Lainey. He reminded Lainey
of the Never doe. Whenever she'd wanted
to go for a run in the forest, she'd given

Lainey a look like that, and Lainey had always understood.

But that was in Never Land, Lainey reminded herself. Here she didn't have animal talent. Still, she couldn't shake the idea that the flamingo was trying to tell her something.

"What is it?" Lainey whispered. She took a step toward the bird. Tentatively, she reached out and touched the flamingo's wing. His feathers felt silky beneath her fingers.

Suddenly, a net swooped down over the flamingo's head. Lainey looked up, startled, and saw Kate gripping the handle of the butterfly net.

"I got him!" Kate cried. "Now he can't get away!"

"Kate, stop! You're scaring him!" Lainey cried as the flamingo began to flail and whip his head.

"*Awnk! Awnk! Awnk!*" Lainey didn't need to have animal talent to know that the bird was upset. She grabbed the net from Kate's hands to set him free.

But at that moment, the flamingo began to run. For such a spindly bird, he was surprisingly strong. Still holding the butterfly net, Lainey was pulled along with it.

"Lainey, let go!" her friends yelled as the bird circled, dragging Lainey behind him.

"I can't!" Lainey cried. The butterfly net seemed to be attached to her arm. She looked and saw a tiny wire loop on the handle. It had gotten hooked on her lasso bracelet.

The flamingo swung around and headed right for the fence. "Stop! Stop!" Lainey screamed. But the bird charged toward the fence at full speed. They were going to crash!

chapter 9

"Ready?" asked Fawn.

Tinker Bell checked the slingshot on her belt, then nodded. "Ready."

That afternoon, Tink and Fawn had carefully made their plan to lure the cat back through the hole to the mainland. Fawn would go first, taunting the cat and leading him toward the hollow tree. Tink would follow her and act as lookout. Queen Clarion had given them both extra fairy dust to help them fly faster.

At the last moment, Tink had tucked the slingshot and a pouch full of peppercorns into her belt. "Just in case," she'd told Fawn.

Fawn eased open the knothole door of the Home Tree and peeked outside. She could see the cat prowling around the roots of the tree.

Fawn took a deep breath. "Hey, fish breath!" she called out in Cat. The cat turned to look. Its eyes lit up at the sight of the fairy.

"Catch me if you can!" cried Fawn, and dove into the air.

The cat leaped after her. To make sure she had him hooked, Fawn led him on a winding chase through Pixie Hollow. First she flew toward the dairy barn. The cat followed closely, as she'd hoped he would.

Just before she reached the barn, Fawn made a hairpin turn and flew in the opposite direction, toward the fairy circle. Glancing over her shoulder, she saw the cat right behind her. His golden eyes were bright with pleasure, as if he was enjoying every moment of the chase.

"Nasty beast," Fawn muttered under her breath. "Only a monster wants to *play* with his lunch before he eats it."

She flew two loops around a hawthorn tree, making sure the cat stayed with her.

"You've got him!" Tink cried from somewhere to her left. "Now go!"

Fawn looped back around and headed toward Havendish Stream and the fairy dust mill. She knew that just beyond, on the far side of the stream, was the hollow fig tree.

"Almost there," Fawn told herself. Soon this whole nightmare would be over. She put on a burst of speed.

But as the tree came into view, Fawn saw something sitting at the mouth of the hollow. As she drew closer, she realized who it was. "Milkweed!"

Hearing his name, the mouse looked up. He wiggled his whiskers in greeting.

Oh no! thought Fawn. If she led the cat to the hollow now, he might go after Milkweed instead. Fawn didn't want to put the mouse in danger. But she couldn't keep

up the chase much longer. For a second, Fawn paused in the air, unsure what to do.

The moment's hesitation was all it took. The cat saw its chance and pounced.

"Fawn!" Tink screamed. "Look out!"

Fawn tried to lurch out of the way, but she was a second too late. The cat's paw struck her. It sent her spinning through the air.

Fawn plummeted toward the ground. She landed in Havendish Stream.

Right away, Fawn knew she was in deep trouble. Like all Never fairies, Fawn couldn't swim. The second she hit the stream, her wings began to soak up water. They started to drag her down.

Just as Fawn's head was about to go under, she felt someone grasp her hand.

Tink was trying to pull her out! Tink fluttered her wings with all her might. As she did, her slingshot came loose from her belt. It landed with a splash next to Fawn's head and sank below the waves.

With her soaked wings, Fawn was too heavy to lift out of the stream. Still gripping Fawn's hand, Tink started to tow her through the water toward shore. At last, she managed to pull her onto the bank.

A shadow fell over them. The fairies looked up and saw the cat closing in.

"Fly!" screamed Tink. Fawn tried to flap her wings, but they felt like sandbags on her back.

The cat loomed over them. The last thing Fawn saw was the cat's lips peeling back from its needle-like teeth.

Fawn closed her eyes. As she braced herself, she heard a booming *"Awnk!"*

Her eyes flew open just in time to see a flamingo burst from the hollow tree. And dragging along behind it was—

"Lainey!" Fawn cried.

If Lainey heard her, Fawn couldn't tell.

The girl's eyes were squeezed tightly shut. Her hair was flying in every direction and her glasses hung from one ear. She clutched the handle of a large net, clinging to it as if for dear life.

chapter 10

"Help!" Lainey cried.

The cat caught one glimpse of the flamingo and turned tail. It sprinted away, yowling in terror.

Suddenly, Lainey felt the flamingo come to a stop beneath her. She slowly peeled open one eye, then the other. She was back in Pixie Hollow!

"Awnk! Awnk!" Lainey heard the voice of another flamingo. She looked around but couldn't see it. Then she spotted Fawn.

The fairy was calling to the bird in its own language, calming it down.

But how did I get here? Lainey wondered. She looked behind her and spotted Kate, Mia, and Gabby climbing out of a hollow tree.

"It's you!" Tinker Bell cried when she saw the girls. "What are you doing here?"

"I don't know!" said Kate, looking equally surprised. "We were in Mia's backyard a second ago. We saw the flamingo pull Lainey through the fence, so we ran to help her—"

"And we ended up here!" Mia broke in. "How did we do that?"

It took a few moments for Fawn, Tink, and the four girls to piece together what had happened. When the flamingo had dragged Lainey toward the fence, the girls had all thought they were going to crash.

"But instead, when they hit the fence, the slat swung sideways and they went right through," said Mia. "So we all followed Lainey, and here we are!"

"There's a loose board," Kate explained.

"And when you go through, you get to Never Land!" Gabby chimed in, not wanting to be left out of the story.

"I still don't understand," said Fawn. "How did you go from the broken fence to the hollow tree?"

Tink tugged her bangs, deep in thought. "The pinprick hole," she said at last.

"The what?" asked Lainey.

Tink explained her theory about the hole between Never Land and the mainland.

"So you mean there's a passage that goes from Pixie Hollow right to Mia and Gabby's backyard?" Kate exclaimed. "That's perfect! Now we can come back whenever we want!"

"It's not perfect," Tink said, her face serious. "In fact, it's very dangerous. We've already had problems. A cat has been on the loose in Pixie Hollow—"

"Did you say a *cat*?" Mia asked.

At that moment, they heard a bell jingling. The sound made Fawn's blood run cold. With a gasp, she turned and saw the cat running toward them.

"Fly, Tink!" Fawn cried. "Don't worry about me! Save yourself!"

But this time the cat barely seemed to notice the fairies. It ran right past Fawn—and straight into Mia's open arms.

"Oh, Bingo! I was so worried about you!" Mia said, rubbing her face in the cat's fluffy fur.

"You . . . *know* this cat?" Fawn asked.

"He's my Bingo," Mia replied, squeezing the cat tightly. "I've been looking all over for him. I was afraid he'd gotten into trouble."

"*Causing* trouble is more like it," Tink said. "He's frightened every fairy in Pixie Hollow. They're all cowering in the Home Tree at this very moment."

Mia lifted Bingo up so they were nose to nose. "Bingo! Bad boy!" she scolded.

Bingo only yawned in reply. "Don't let him fool you," Mia told the fairies. "He

may pretend to be tough, but he wouldn't hurt a fly. He just wants to play."

"To play?" Fawn echoed faintly. "You mean, the cat has only been trying to play with us this whole time?"

Mia nodded. "I know he can be a bit rough, but it's not his fault. He's still just a baby—not much older than a kitten. He loves to have fun."

Tink rolled her eyes. "Some kind of fun."

The sound of another bell made everyone turn. A little gray mouse was making his way toward them.

"Milkweed!" Lainey cried in relief. She picked him up. Lainey watched the mouse sniff the palm of her hand. She knew she needed to tell Fawn the truth—that she didn't really have animal talent.

She wondered if Fawn would still want to be her friend.

"I lost Milkweed on the mainland," Lainey confessed to Fawn. "I thought I'd lost him for good. I couldn't communicate with him at all—or with the dog or any other animals. I don't really have animal talent," she added. "At home, I'm not really good at anything. I'm just a regular old Clumsy."

"Oh, Lainey," Fawn said. "Animal talent doesn't come and go. It's something in your heart. And you have a very big heart. That's even more important than being able to speak to animals. Speaking isn't everything—even I sometimes misunderstand," she added with a glance at Bingo.

"So you still want to be my friend?" Lainey asked.

"Of course," said Fawn. She was too tiny to hug Lainey, so she hugged her thumb.

Lainey felt better. "And now I can come visit you any time!" she said. "All we have to do is go through the fence."

"What *are* you going to do about the hole?" Kate asked Tinker Bell. "You're not going to close it up, I hope?"

"I wouldn't even begin to know how," Tink replied. She tugged her bangs, thinking. "Still, the hole is a danger. We have to do something. We'll start with telling Queen Clarion."

"Why don't you come with us?" Fawn said to the girls. "All the fairies are in the Home Tree right now. They'll be so glad to see you. Lainey, my wings are too wet to fly. Will you carry me?"

Together the girls and the fairies set off for the Home Tree. Lainey was filled with pride carrying Fawn on her shoulder. There were so many questions still to be answered—about the hole in the fence that led to Never Land and

whether she had animal talent. But one thing no longer bothered her. Lainey was certain now that she was special. For, she thought, there was nothing more special in the world than being a fairy's friend.

How sad, Mia thought,
not to be able to see magic
even when it's right
in front of your eyes.

THE NEVER GIRLS

a
dandelion
wish

Written by
Kiki Thorpe

Illustrated by
Jana Christy

A STEPPING STONE BOOK™

RANDOM HOUSE 🏠 NEW YORK

Chapter 1

Mia Vasquez awoke Saturday morning with a fluttery feeling in her chest. A feeling that something great awaited her that day.

She rubbed her eyes, trying to recall what it was. Then she remembered: *Never Land.*

The two words sent her leaping from her bed. She ran to the window and looked out at the backyard. White clouds chased each other across the blue sky. The grass was tall and the flowers bloomed in their beds. But it was the high wooden fence that held Mia's attention.

The day before, Mia, her little sister, Gabby, and her friends Kate and Lainey had discovered that by crawling through a loose board in the fence, they could reach the magical island of Never Land. No one knew how the passage between the two worlds had come to be—not even the fairies whose magic had brought the girls to Never Land in the first place. But to Mia it was a dream come true. To think she could visit the fairy world anytime she wanted, just by going through the fence in her own backyard!

Mia dressed quickly in a polka-dotted skirt and her favorite pink T-shirt. Her long, curly black hair fell over her shoulders. She considered a pretty pair of sandals, then pulled on her sneakers instead. Sneakers were better for adventures—and there were always adventures to be had in Never Land.

When she was dressed, Mia hurried downstairs to the kitchen. She poured herself a bowl of cereal and slid into a chair next to her little sister. Gabby was wearing a pink tutu and a pair of costume fairy wings—her everyday outfit. She was drawing a picture of a fairy with crayons.

The girls' mother was standing at the kitchen counter, drinking a cup of coffee. "That's a nice drawing, Gabby," she said. "What's the fairy's name?"

"That's Tinker Bell," Gabby said. "She lives in Pixie Hollow."

Mrs. Vasquez smiled. "Where is that?"

"It's on the other side of the— Ow! Mia!" Gabby exclaimed as Mia kicked her under the table. When she caught Gabby's eye, Mia frowned and shook her head. Their parents didn't know about Never Land, and Mia didn't want them to find out. She had a feeling that if they did, the girls' adventuring would be over.

Out the kitchen window, Mia could see her father working in the yard. She hoped he would be done soon. Otherwise, they couldn't sneak through the fence.

"Is Papi going to be doing yard work for long?" Mia asked her mother casually. "Kate and Lainey are coming over. We were going to, um . . . play outside."

"Your friends can't come over today, Mia," her mother said. "I'm going out to do some errands, and I need you to look after Gabby."

"What? But I already told them they could come!" Mia cried.

"You'll have to call them and tell them they can't," her mother replied.

And not go to Never Land? Mia couldn't bear the thought. "Can't they come over anyway?" she asked. "We can all watch Gabby together."

"No, Mia," said her mom. "If you get busy playing with your friends, you'll forget to keep an eye on Gabby."

"I wouldn't!" Mia said. She thought of the first time they'd found themselves in Never Land, pulled there on a fairy's blink. Hadn't she and her friends taken good care of Gabby then? But, of course, she couldn't point this out to her mother.

"Kate and Lainey can come over another time," Mrs. Vasquez said.

"It's not fair!" Mia complained. "Papi's here. Why can't he watch Gabby?"

"Papi is busy today. Mia, please don't sulk. It's just one day. You're old enough to be responsible."

"Who cares about being responsible?" Mia grumbled under her breath. She watched, arms folded, as her mother picked up her purse and left.

When she was gone, Mia called Kate and Lainey and told them they couldn't come over. Then she returned to the table, plopped herself down in a chair, and glared at her sister.

Gabby didn't seem to notice. "Do you want to play a game?"

"No," Mia snapped.

"Do you want to color?" asked Gabby.

Mia's frown deepened. "No. Why don't you go watch TV or something?"

"I'm not supposed to watch TV unless Mami says it's okay," Gabby pointed out.

"Well, I'm in charge today, and *I* say it's okay," Mia replied.

At once, Gabby hopped up from the table. She ran into the living room. A moment later, Mia heard the TV turn on.

With nothing better to do, Mia followed her into the living room. She flopped down on the sofa. On the television screen, a bunch of cartoon monsters were singing a silly song.

Mia sighed. She couldn't think of anything more frustrating than to be stuck watching a lame kiddie show when she could be spending time with *real* fairies.

She looked out the living room window at the high wooden fence. Never Land lay just on the other side. She could reach it in less than thirty seconds.

Well, why shouldn't I? Mia thought. *I could just pop over and see what's going on in Pixie Hollow. I'll be back before anyone even knows I'm gone.*

Mia glanced at her sister. Gabby was

caught up in her cartoon. *She'll be fine for a few minutes,* Mia thought.

Quietly, she slipped off the couch and let herself out the back door.

She didn't see her father, but she could hear him whistling. He was working somewhere around the side of the house. Now was her chance.

The loose board was on the fence that separated the yard from their neighbor's. Mia had to spend a few moments nudging the boards until she found the right one. The board swung sideways on its nail, creating a gap just big enough for her to squeeze through.

As Mia knelt down, she felt a warm breeze on her face. She could smell jasmine and sun-warmed moss—the sweet scent of Pixie Hollow. She took a deep breath, then crawled through the opening, pulling the board back into place behind her.

*

She came out from a hollow tree into a sun-dappled forest. To her left was a wildflower-filled meadow. To her right, Havendish Stream burbled between its banks. And just beyond the stream lay Pixie Hollow. Mia could see fairies darting through the air as they flew to and from the giant Home Tree.

Mia heard a commotion downstream. She followed the sound around a bend, to a small wooden bridge. Dozens of fairies swarmed around the bridge. They carried rope and bits of wood and buckets full of sand.

Mia saw Tinker Bell flying past. "Hi, Tink. What's going on?" she asked.

"The footbridge is out," Tink replied. Now Mia saw that part of the bridge had collapsed into the stream. "We think Bingo must have smashed it when he was chasing fairies."

"Oh no!" Bingo was Mia's cat. The day before, he'd slipped through the fence into Never Land and caused trouble. "Can you fix it?"

"Yes, but it will take a lot of work," Tink said happily. "I'd better get back." She waved to Mia and flew off. Tink was always happiest when she had something to fix.

The fairies at the bridge all seemed busy, so Mia decided to go to the Home Tree. Perhaps she could find someone to talk to there.

In the pebbled courtyard, Mia saw

sweeping-talent fairies tidying up. They waved to Mia, but kept on with their jobs. It was the same in the kitchen. When Mia peered through the tiny doorway, the cooking- and baking-talent fairies barely looked up.

"Busy day in Pixie Hollow," said the baking fairy Dulcie as she rolled out pie dough. "Lots of hungry fairies to feed."

Mia was disappointed. She'd hoped she might come upon a tea party or a game of fairy tag. But everyone in Pixie Hollow was hard at work. Mia wondered if she should help—after all, it was her cat that had caused the mess. But she knew she shouldn't leave Gabby alone for too long. Time worked differently in Never Land, and Mia couldn't be sure if a minute or an hour had gone by since she had left.

As Mia started back, she passed a tiny house made from a gourd that sat on one of the Home Tree's lowest branches. She tapped on the little wooden door with her finger.

The garden fairy Rosetta opened the door. She was dressed in a glorious ruffled gown made from a pink carnation. "Mia!" Rosetta exclaimed. "I was hoping someone might drop by. I'm glad it's you!"

"Are you going to a party?" Mia asked hopefully, eyeing Rosetta's fancy dress.

Rosetta sighed sadly. "No parties today—not even a picnic. Everyone is too busy cleaning up after . . . well, you know, what happened with Bingo."

"Why aren't you busy, too?" asked Mia.

"Well, Bingo made a great mess of almost everything, but he left all the flowers alone. There's not much for a garden fairy to do. So I've been trying on dresses. Sometimes I do that when I'm feeling bored," Rosetta admitted. "But now I'm out of dresses—I've tried on everything!"

Suddenly, Mia had an idea. It was such a good idea that she wondered why she hadn't thought of it before. "Why don't you come to my house? I have lots of dresses that would fit you perfectly," she said, thinking of her doll clothes.

"You mean, go through the fig tree to the mainland? I don't know." Rosetta suddenly looked nervous. "Some fairies say it's dangerous."

Mia laughed. "It's not dangerous. I just came through it! Rosetta, you have to come. I have a pink velvet dress that would look beautiful on you. Oh! And one made of blue lace. And a green one with a little matching bag . . ."

As Mia described the dresses, Rosetta's blue eyes widened. At last, she burst out, "I'd love to see them all!"

"Come on. Let's go right now," said Mia.

With Rosetta flying beside her, Mia led the way back to the hollow tree. She was thrilled. This was the perfect answer to her problem. She could look after Gabby and still have fun!

But when they got to the tree, Rosetta hesitated. "Are you sure it's safe?" she asked.

"You can ride in my pocket, if it makes you feel better," Mia said.

Rosetta flew into Mia's pocket. Then Mia crawled into the hollow tree, and back to her own world.

Chapter 2

As Mia came back through the fence into her yard, she could still hear her father whistling from somewhere around the side of the house. *Good,* Mia thought. That meant she'd only been gone for a few moments.

Quickly, Mia crossed the yard and went in the back door to the house. "I'll be in my room, Gabby," she said as she passed the living room.

Gabby looked up from the TV. "What's that?" she asked, eyeing the lump in Mia's pocket.

"Nothing. Mind your own business," Mia said, hurrying up the stairs to her room.

In the hallway, Bingo was prowling. When he saw Mia, he wrapped himself around her legs and purred. Inside Mia's pocket, Rosetta tensed.

"Go away, Bingo." Mia nudged the cat gently with her foot. She slipped past him into her room, quickly shutting the door behind her. On the other side, Bingo yowled in protest.

"It's okay," Mia said to Rosetta. "You can come out now."

Rosetta wriggled out of the pocket. "Phew!" She fluffed her long red hair.

Then her eyes widened, and she gave a little gasp. "Oh my!"

Mia glanced around, seeing her room through Rosetta's eyes. Instantly, she regretted not making her bed that morning. And all those clothes on the floor—why hadn't she noticed them until now?

Mia hastily scooped up socks and T-shirts, throwing them in the hamper, and yanked the purple coverlet up over her bed. But when Mia glanced back at Rosetta, she realized the fairy wasn't looking at the mess. She was staring, transfixed, at the corner of the room, where a large dollhouse stood.

Rosetta flew over and landed in the dollhouse's living room. She examined the little sofa, the miniature grandfather clock, and the postage-stamp pictures on the walls. Her fairy glow cast a warm light over the small room, making it look as if the dollhouse lamps were lit.

Moving from room to room, Rosetta explored the rest of the dollhouse. She touched the tiny china teacups in the dining room. She opened the oven door in the kitchen. She even stretched out on the canopy bed in the guest bedroom.

Mia's breath caught in delight. She had always liked playing with her dollhouse, but it had never been more than a pretty toy. The moment the fairy stepped inside, though, the house came to life.

"Who lives here?" Rosetta asked.

"No one," Mia replied. "It's . . . just for fun."

"Just for fun?" Rosetta cried in surprise. "But it's a perfect home for a fairy!"

Mia grinned, imagining a fairy living in her dollhouse.

At that moment, the door to Mia's room burst open. Gabby stood in the doorway. "I knew it!" she crowed, spying Rosetta. "I knew you had a fairy here!"

"Gabby!" cried Mia. "You're supposed to knock!"

Gabby ignored her. She barged into the room. "What are you guys playing? Can I play, too? Will you come to my room, Rosetta? I want to show you my toys and my books and my stuffed animals. Can you come right now? Can you?"

Mia grabbed hold of her sister by one wing and spun her around. "Out!" she exclaimed. "Get out of my room!"

"Let go, Mia!" Gabby shouted.

"It's all right, Mia," Rosetta said. She flew out of the dollhouse, which became just an ordinary toy once again.

"No, it's not," Mia said. "It's my room, and I didn't invite Gabby in. She's *intruding*." Mia knew she was being mean, but she couldn't stop herself. Gabby was the reason she was stuck at home and not in Never Land. Even though Mia knew it wasn't Gabby's fault, she couldn't help being mad at her.

As the sisters glared at each other, a blur of brown fur streaked into the room through the open door.

"Bingo!" the girls shrieked. They dove for the cat at the same time. Their heads collided with a loud smack. Bingo shot past them, headed right for Rosetta.

The fairy screamed and darted into the air. Bingo leaped onto Mia's dresser. He stood on his hind legs, batting the air as he tried to reach the fairy.

Gabby jumped up to grab him, but she wasn't quite tall enough. Instead, she knocked Mia's jewelry box off the dresser. The box crashed to the floor, and the hinges broke. All the trinkets inside scattered.

"Gabby!" Mia wailed. "Bingo!" She didn't know who to yell at first. She snatched the cat off her dresser and tucked him under her arm. Then she clamped her other hand down on Gabby's shoulder, steering her toward the door. "Both of you—out!"

"I want to stay!" Gabby said, digging in her heels.

"No. You mess up *everything*," Mia said. She pushed Gabby and Bingo into the hall and locked the door behind them.

"Fine! Then I'll do something fun in *my* room. And *you're* not invited!" Gabby shouted through the door.

"Fine with me!" Mia shouted back.

Gabby stomped away. A second later, Mia heard her bedroom door slam.

"I don't think she meant to let Bingo in," Rosetta said, fluttering down from the ceiling.

Mia touched her head. It throbbed where she'd run into Gabby. "You don't know what it's like to have a little sister," she told Rosetta. "Gabby's always getting in the way."

"Maybe I should go home," the fairy said. She looked nervous, and Mia realized she was still afraid of Bingo.

"Don't leave yet!" Mia begged. If Rosetta left now, the whole day would be ruined. "I haven't even shown you the dresses!"

Mia hurried to her closet and pulled out the two shoe boxes where she kept her doll clothes. She lifted the lids and began laying the dresses out one by one.

Pink, yellow, green, gold. Satin, taffeta, and lace. Some of the dresses were trimmed with ribbon. Others were bursting with petticoats. Still others had matching cloaks and hats.

Rosetta came closer, lured by the lovely clothes. "Look how many there are!"

"Try one on," Mia urged.

"All right. Just one." After much

consideration, Rosetta selected a ruffled
pink dress with a gold sash.

The dress fit perfectly. Rosetta flew
back and forth in front of Mia's dresser
mirror, admiring herself. Mia clapped
her hands. The dress had never looked
this pretty on her dolls. "Try this one

next!" she urged, holding up a yellow ball gown.

Rosetta tried on dress after dress. Mia thought each one looked lovelier than the last. She was having so much fun she didn't notice the time passing.

Bang! Bang! Bang! A pounding sound from outside startled Mia.

"What was that?" asked Rosetta.

"I don't know." Suddenly, Mia thought of Gabby. How long had it been since she'd seen her? "I'll be right back," she told Rosetta.

Mia went across the hall. But Gabby's room was empty. Downstairs, the television was still on, but Gabby wasn't watching. She wasn't in the kitchen or the bathroom, either.

Mia went back to her room. "I can't find her," she told Rosetta.

"Who?" asked the fairy. She had on a green satin dress and was admiring herself in the mirror.

"Gabby!" exclaimed Mia. "She's not anywhere in the house."

Rosetta looked at her. "Where else could she be?"

With a sinking feeling, Mia suddenly knew exactly where her sister was. Gabby had gone through the fence into Pixie Hollow.

"Gabby, you're such a pest," she grumbled to herself. But she hurried down the stairs. It was one thing for Mia to go to Never Land on her own. But Gabby was just a little girl. Who knew what kind of trouble she could get into?

When she stepped outside, Mia spotted Gabby's sweatshirt, the one she'd been wearing that morning. It was lying on the ground near the fence. Mia knew then that she was right. Gabby must have taken it off right before she went through the hole.

Mia saw her father standing at the fence. He had a hammer in his hand. But what was he doing?

As Mia watched, her father brought the hammer down on the fence. *Bang! Bang! Bang!*

"Oh no!" Mia cried. Her father was fixing the hole in the fence—and Gabby was on the other side!

Chapter 3

Iridessa, a light-talent fairy, knelt before a pool of sunlight. She reached into the pool and pulled out a sunbeam. Her hands shaped the sunbeam into a ball, like a golden glowing pearl. Then she placed it in her basket.

Iridessa sat back on her heels and eyed the basket of sunbeams. It was almost full. *Is that enough?* she wondered.

Better get a few more, she decided. In Iridessa's opinion, it was always better to be safe than sorry. With the bridge builders working through the night, Pixie Hollow would need extra light.

As soon as she was done collecting sunbeams, she needed to round up more fireflies. There was so much to do! Luckily, Iridessa had made a plan for the day. She glanced up at the sun high in the sky and smiled. She was right on schedule.

Iridessa reached into the pool again. But just as her fingers touched it, a shadow fell over her. She turned.

A giant loomed above. Iridessa noticed that it had wings—and a tutu. "Gabby?" she said.

"Hi, Iridessa." The girl squatted down next to her. "Will you come to my room? I'm having a party."

"Now?" Iridessa wondered why anyone would have a party at such a busy time.

"Everyone is invited—except Mia," Gabby told her.

Suddenly, Iridessa understood. "Did you have a fight with your sister?"

Gabby's forehead furrowed. "She won't let me play with her and Rosetta. And she yelled at me, even though it wasn't my fault about Bingo. And she made me leave. She pulled my wings! She's mean!"

Iridessa didn't know what to make of all this. But she did know what it was like to be mad at someone. "Perhaps she wasn't mean on purpose," she said.

"She was so," said Gabby. "I never want to see her again."

"Come now," said Iridessa. "There must be something you like about your sister."

Gabby shook her head.

"Think hard," Iridessa urged. "Just one thing."

Gabby considered. "Well, sometimes she lets me watch TV."

"What is that?" asked the fairy.

Gabby looked at her in amazement. "It's . . . TV!"

Some quaint Clumsy custom, no doubt, thought Iridessa. "Well, imagine if you didn't have your sister *or* TV. Wouldn't that be sad?"

"I guess so," said Gabby.

"I'll bet if you remind Mia how much you like it when you watch TV, it will make her feel happy. And then you two can make up," Iridessa said.

"Do you really think so?" Gabby asked.

"Yes," said Iridessa. "People always like to hear good things about themselves. Sometimes the best way to get over an argument is to remember the nice things about each other. You should talk to Mia. Come on, I'll take you back to the hollow tree."

Iridessa picked up her basket of sunbeams. This wasn't part of her day's plan.

But she was glad to help. Iridessa liked to see things sorted out. And it had only taken her—Iridessa glanced at the sun—forty-seven seconds!

She led Gabby across the meadow, back to the tree that held the portal to the girls' world. Iridessa stopped at the entrance to the hollow.

"Fly safely," she said, in the fairy manner.

"Okay." Gabby turned and ducked into the hollow. A second later, she came right back out.

"What's wrong?" Iridessa asked.

"The hole isn't there," said Gabby.

"Of course it is," Iridessa replied. "You came through it earlier, didn't you?"

Gabby nodded. "But now it's gone."

Iridessa thought Gabby must be mistaken. She set down her basket and flew into the tree. It was dark inside the hollow, but all fairies glow a little and Iridessa's glow was stronger than most. She could see the inside walls of the hollow, smooth and unbroken.

"It's gone! The portal's gone!" Iridessa exclaimed, flying out of the tree.

"I told you," said Gabby.

"What should I do?" Iridessa asked. This was important news! But whether it was good or bad news, Iridessa wasn't certain. She fluttered back and forth. She sometimes got flustered when things didn't work out as planned.

Just then, a messenger-talent fairy flew by. Iridessa zipped over and told her what they'd discovered. Within moments, the messenger spread the news around Pixie Hollow. Fairies and sparrow men all stopped what they were doing. They came to examine the tree.

"So it's true?" asked Queen Clarion, flying up.

"It is," said Tinker Bell, who'd been inspecting the tree. "The hollow is still there. But the portal has vanished!"

As the fairies buzzed with the news, Iridessa's eyes darted to Gabby. The girl stood off to the side, watching the fairies silently. She seemed to be waiting to be told what to do. The other fairies barely noticed her, however. They were all focused on the tree.

Iridessa flew over to Queen Clarion. "What about Gabby?" she murmured.

"She can't get home. Someone will need to look after her."

The queen rubbed a hand across her forehead. She looked distracted. "Yes, you're right, of course. That's very good of you, Iridessa."

"What? Oh! No." Iridessa shook her head and tried to explain. "That's not what I meant. . . ." But the queen was already flying away.

Iridessa sighed. She had sunbeams to collect and fireflies to gather. Looking after a Clumsy was *not* part of her plan.

She flew back over to Gabby. "Don't worry," she said brightly. "I'm sure the hole will open again in no time." Iridessa wasn't sure of any such thing. But she didn't want Gabby to worry.

In the meantime, she had no choice. If she was going to stick to her plan, she'd just have to bring Gabby along with her.

Well, she's only a young girl, after all, she thought. *How hard can it be to look after her?*

chapter 4

Mia ran toward her father, crying, "Papi, wait!"

Mr. Vasquez looked up. "Mia?"

When she reached the fence, Mia ran her fingers along it. None of the boards budged. "There was a loose board!"

"I know, I fixed it," her father replied. "I've been meaning to repair this old fence for ages. You don't know what might get through a hole like that. Stray dogs or cats or— Mia, honey, what's the matter?"

"Gabby is . . ." Mia trailed off, her mind racing.

What if she told her father about Never Land? What would happen? Would he tell other grown-ups about the fairy world? Would he leave the hole sealed up for good? Would he even believe her?

Mia didn't know. But one thing was certain—if her parents found out she'd lost track of Gabby, she was going to be in big trouble.

Her father frowned. "Gabby is what?"

"Sleeping," Mia said quickly, making a decision. "She's taking a nap. I was afraid the hammering would wake her up."

"Well, I'm done here." Her father picked up his tools. "I've got some work to do in the garage. *Quiet* work," he added with a wink. Then he patted Mia's cheek. "You're a good big sister."

A guilty lump rose in Mia's throat. She swallowed hard, forcing it down. *It's not my fault,* Mia told herself. *If Gabby hadn't left without telling me, this wouldn't have happened!*

When her father was gone, Mia turned back to the fence. She tried wiggling the wooden boards. She tried kicking them. Not one of them budged.

"Stupid fence!" Mia exclaimed, giving it an extra kick.

"Mia?" said a voice behind her.

Mia turned and saw Rosetta hovering. She was still wearing the green satin doll dress. "What's going on?" the fairy asked.

Gabby wasn't the only one who was trapped in the wrong world, Mia realized. Rosetta was stuck, too!

But unlike Gabby, Rosetta had magic. Maybe she could help. "Papi fixed the fence. But Gabby is in Never Land, and now she can't get home!" Mia explained. "Can you do something?"

"You mean, the way back to Never Land is gone?" Rosetta's face turned pale. Her eyelids fluttered. Mia stuck out her hand just in time to catch her as she fainted.

*

Inside the house, Mia ran a washrag under the kitchen tap. Carefully, she squeezed a drop of water onto Rosetta's forehead.

The fairy spluttered and sat up. When she saw Mia's giant face hovering over her, she screamed.

"Sorry!" Mia backed away quickly. "I didn't mean to scare you."

Rosetta put a hand to her cheek. "What happened?"

"You fainted when I told you we can't get back to Never Land," Mia said.

Rosetta looked like she might faint again, so Mia made her comfortable on a dry kitchen sponge.

"That's better. A cup of tea would be nice, too," Rosetta said.

Mia didn't know how to make tea. But she wanted Rosetta to feel better. She fetched a doll's teacup from her room and put a drop of soda in it, then handed it to the fairy.

Rosetta took one sip and yelped. "It burns! But it's cold!"

"It's root beer," said Mia.

Rosetta drained her cup and smacked her lips. "Have you got a little something to go with it? A poppy-seed thimblecake, perhaps? With a dollop of fresh cream and a sprinkle of pollen?"

Mia studied the cupboard. "We have crackers."

As she handed one to Rosetta, the doorbell rang. Mia ran to answer it. Her best friend, Kate McCrady, was standing on the doorstep. Mia had called Kate and Lainey for help. She remembered what

her mother had said about not having her friends over. But this was an emergency.

"You said to come over. Then you said not to come over. Then you said, 'Come over—and hurry!' Make up your mind, Mia!" Kate joked.

Mia didn't feel like laughing. She led Kate into the kitchen. Rosetta was still sitting on the counter, making her way through an oyster cracker.

"What are you doing here?" Kate cried when she saw Rosetta. "Aren't we going to Never Land today?"

"Well, that's the thing. . . ." Mia started to explain how Rosetta had ended up on the mainland. But right away Kate interrupted.

"Wait a minute. You mean, you went

to Never Land *without* me?" Kate looked both annoyed and envious.

"Don't be mad, Kate," Mia pleaded. "I've got a big problem. Gabby is stuck in Never Land!"

"She went, too? So much for sticking with your friends," Kate grumbled.

To Mia's relief, the doorbell rang again. This time it was Lainey Winters. Her blond hair was uncombed and her glasses were slightly crooked on her face. "I came as fast as I could," she said breathlessly.

The girls listened as Mia explained how Gabby had come to be trapped in Never Land, and Rosetta stuck in their world.

"Can't you do anything?" Lainey asked Rosetta. "I mean, with fairy magic?"

"Nope, I already asked," Mia told her.

Rosetta lifted her chin. "I'm a garden fairy," she said proudly. "Holes aren't one of my talents. Our magic is different. I can make any flower bloom. I can hear the secrets inside a seed."

Kate rolled her eyes. "A lot of good that will do us."

"You said your dad nailed the board shut," Lainey said, thinking. "So really all we need to do is loosen it again."

"It's nailed down tight," Mia said. "But we can try."

The group hurried outside to study the fence. "Which board was it?" Rosetta asked.

"It was somewhere in the middle," said Mia.

"I thought it was closer to the right," said Kate.

"How can you tell?" asked Lainey. "They all look the same!"

Kate folded her arms across her chest. "Mia should know. *She* was the last one through it," she said, giving Mia a meaningful look.

"Kate, I said I was sorry!" Mia wailed.

"Actually, you didn't," Kate replied.

Mia sighed. "I'm sorry I went to Never Land without you. Will you please stop being mad now?"

"Maybe," Kate said with a smile. She kicked at a few fence boards. "Well, since we can't remember which board it is, I guess we're just going to have to try them all."

"You mean, loosen every board?" Mia was horrified. "What are my parents going to think?"

"What are they going to think when you tell them Gabby sneaked off to the magical island of Never Land while you were supposed to be watching her?" Kate asked pointedly. "Mia, it's the only way."

"Fine." Mia scowled. "I can't wait to get Gabby back . . . so I can yell at her."

Kate knelt down and began to wiggle a board. "It's really nailed tight. Ow!" She jerked back her hand. "I got a splinter."

Rosetta fluttered over to her. "Let me see it."

"Do you have healing magic?" Kate asked, holding out her thumb.

"No, but I have tiny hands." Rosetta landed on Kate's palm and began to gently work out the splinter.

That gave Mia an idea. "I know! We need something to pull the nails out." She ran into the house and returned a few moments later with a hammer.

Using the claw end of the hammer, Mia began to wiggle the nail from the wood. "Just a little more . . . there!" Mia pulled out the nail, then pushed the board to one side, just enough so she could peek through. "I see flowers. And I can hear water running."

"That must be Havendish Stream!" Rosetta cried joyously. "Oh, I'll be back in time for tea!" She zipped right past Mia and through the gap in the fence.

At that moment, a large shape crossed in front of the gap, blocking Mia's view. She heard someone grumbling. But it didn't sound like a fairy's voice. It sounded like a grown-up.

That's not Pixie Hollow! Mia realized with a gasp. It was her neighbor Mrs. Peavy's yard—and that large shape blocking her view was Mrs. Peavy herself. Rosetta had flown right into the old woman's garden!

"What's wrong, Mia?" Kate asked behind her.

"We got the wrong board." Mia put her eye back to the crack, but she couldn't see the fairy. "Rosetta, come back!" she whispered.

There was no reply.

Mia watched through the crack. She could see Mrs. Peavy's feet. The old woman stood still for a long time. She seemed to be looking at something.

Mia's heart beat faster. Had Mrs. Peavy found Rosetta?

The old woman turned and walked back toward her house.

As soon as she was gone, Mia whispered louder, "Rosetta, are you okay?"

Silence.

Mia felt panic rising in her chest. "We have to go in there!" she cried. "Something happened to Rosetta!"

(hapter 5

"What do you know about spotting fireflies?" Iridessa asked Gabby.

The two were making their way through the forest just outside Pixie Hollow. Iridessa flew in front of Gabby, leading the way through the moss-covered trees.

"They have lights in their bottoms," Gabby replied.

"That's right," said Iridessa. "But they can be hard to see in the daytime. That's why we need a plan. We should start by looking for puddles. Then we move on to shady thickets. Then we'll go— Are you listening, Gabby? Gabby?"

Iridessa turned. The little girl had vanished.

Iridessa hovered, looking around. *She's ten times the size of a fairy,* she thought. *How is it possible that I've lost her already?*

"BOO!" Gabby yelled, springing up from behind a bush. Iridessa was so startled that she fell from the air. She landed in a giant fern.

Gabby giggled. "I scared you!"

Iridessa could barely conceal her annoyance. "Gabby, we don't have time for games. Just stay close, now."

This time Iridessa flew behind so she could keep an eye on Gabby. But it wasn't easy. The little girl was all over the place! She'd stop to admire a fuzzy caterpillar. Then suddenly, she'd dash off to examine a mushroom or peek into a hollow log.

"It's harder than herding a butterfly!" Iridessa groaned.

Before she could stop her, Gabby darted away again. In an instant, she had vanished among the trees.

At last, Iridessa spotted the tips of Gabby's wings poking out from behind a mossy oak. "What are you up to now?" she asked, flying over.

Gabby was holding a silver dandelion.
Iridessa watched as she closed her eyes
and blew away all the seeds with a single breath. Ever since they'd entered the
forest, Gabby had stopped to pick every

dandelion she'd seen. It was starting to drive Iridessa crazy.

"Why do you do that?" she asked.

"For a wish," Gabby said.

"On a dandelion?" Iridessa had never heard of such a thing.

"When you wish on a dandelion, a fairy hears your wish and makes it come true," Gabby replied. "That's what Mia says."

Iridessa frowned. Never fairies didn't grant wishes. In Iridessa's opinion, *planning* was how you went about making sure things turned out as you wanted. *What a lot of silly ideas Clumsies have,* she thought.

Suddenly, Gabby's eyes lit up. "Ooh, look! A firefly!" She pointed at a glimmer of light ahead in the trees.

A single firefly wasn't worth the trouble of chasing, Iridessa thought. But Gabby was already darting after it. "It's not— Wait! Come back!" Iridessa cried.

Gabby scrambled over rocks and under branches, grabbing for the firefly that was always out of reach. Iridessa was surprised at how fast the girl could run. She could barely keep up.

In moments, they were deep in the woods. The trees grew close together. But it wasn't just the trees blocking out the light—the whole forest seemed to be growing darker, almost as if night was coming on.

That can't be right, Iridessa thought. *Sunset is hours away.*

She glanced up at the sky. Between the towering trees, she could see thunderheads gathering. Storms were rare in Never Land. But they did happen.

Suddenly, Iridessa felt worried. She put on a burst of speed to catch up with Gabby. "Don't go so far. We need to . . ."

Iridessa trailed off, forgetting the rest of her thought. Gabby was standing in the center of a clearing, surrounded by thousands of fireflies. They wove patterns in the air around her. The little girl danced with joy.

Iridessa lived in an enchanted world, but even to her, the scene was like magic. She'd never seen so many fireflies glowing so brightly. For just one moment, Iridessa forgot about her plan and her schedule. She didn't even think of trying to herd all

the fireflies. Instead, she flew up next to Gabby. Together, they laughed and danced as the fireflies swirled around them.

Then, all at once, the lights winked out.

"What happened?" Gabby asked.

"Something scared them off," Iridessa replied, looking around.

CRRACK! There came a clap of thunder so loud Iridessa felt it in her bones. The sky opened up, and rain poured down. It came so hard and fast that it washed Iridessa right out of the air.

The fairy landed hard on the muddy ground. She tried to stand and run for shelter. But before she could, a rivulet of water picked her up and swept her away.

Iridessa bounced over the ground, carried by the water. She grabbed at roots and blades of grass, trying to hold on. But the water tore her off. It swept up everything in its path. Leaves and sticks slammed against her. The forest spun above her. She was going to drown!

Suddenly, a hand grabbed her roughly and lifted her into the air. Iridessa found herself looking into a pair of wide brown eyes.

"Gabby!" Iridessa was so relieved she could have cried.

"Are you okay?" the girl asked.

Iridessa nodded. She was muddy and bruised. Her wings were too wet to fly. But she wasn't badly hurt.

Cradling Iridessa in her hands, Gabby ducked under a giant fern. They waited out the storm. It didn't last long. Almost as quickly as it had come, the rain cleared up.

Iridessa fanned her wet wings, trying to dry them. "We'd better go back to Pixie Hollow before we get caught in another storm," she told Gabby. "You'll have to carry me for now. I can't fly with wet wings."

"Okay," said Gabby. "Which way do we go?"

"This way." Iridessa pointed into the trees. "No . . . that doesn't look right. Is it this way?" She spun in a circle. But each way she turned, the trees looked the same.

With a sinking feeling, Iridessa realized they were lost.

chapter 6

"Are you sure about this, Kate?" Lainey asked.

Kate was using the hammer to work another nail loose from the fence board. "How else are we going to get into the garden to find Rosetta?" she asked.

"We could ring Mrs. Peavy's doorbell," Lainey suggested. "We could say we lost a ball in her yard."

"She'll never let us in," Mia said. "She doesn't even answer the door for trick-or-treaters. On Halloween, she turns off all the lights and closes her drapes."

"I heard she's a witch," Lainey whispered.

"I heard that, too," said Mia.

Kate frowned. "I thought witches were supposed to love Halloween." She pulled the nail out. Pushing the board sideways made a gap just big enough to squeeze through.

The girls all looked at each other. "Who's going?" asked Kate. For the first time in her life, she didn't look eager to have an adventure.

"Let's do rock-paper-scissors," Mia suggested. "On the count of three. One . . . two . . . three!"

Mia scissored her fingers. Kate and Lainey both curled their fists into rocks.

Mia swallowed hard. "Okay," she said. "Wish me luck."

"Good luck," said Lainey.

"Don't get turned into a frog," said Kate.

Mia scowled at her, then crawled through the fence.

She found herself in an overgrown garden. The grass grew a foot high and the flower beds were choked with weeds. The few flowers that remained were wilted, and the herbs had all gone to seed. The sole tree in the garden was so strangled by ivy that Mia couldn't see an inch of its bark.

It sure looks *like a witch's garden,* Mia thought. She glanced up at the house, but the shades were drawn. Was it possible that Rosetta was trapped inside?

Mia tiptoed farther into the garden.

Just then, she spotted her friend. The fairy was crouched beside a bedraggled rosebush. It looked as if she was talking to it.

Mia hurried over. "There you are! We thought something happened to you. We were so worried!"

Rosetta looked up at her with tears in her eyes. "Mia, look at this place. Who would do this to a garden? Flowers need love and care. You can't just *ignore* them."

Mia was getting anxious. Mrs. Peavy could come back any minute. "We should go now," she whispered.

"But, Mia," Rosetta said, widening her eyes. "I can't *leave* them like this!"

"You there!" a gravelly voice rang out, making Mia's blood run cold. "What are you doing in my garden?"

Mia turned and saw Mrs. Peavy standing a few feet away. The woman was wearing a wide-brimmed hat that cast a shadow over the top half of her face, so Mia couldn't see her eyes. But her mouth was turned down in a deep frown. She gripped a gardening trowel in her fist as if it were a weapon.

Mia's lips moved, but no words came out. They seemed to be stuck in her throat.

"Speak up!" Mrs. Peavy came closer. Now Mia could see her eyes. They were a startling shade of blue.

"Who were you talking to?" the woman snapped. "And don't lie to me. I can smell a lie a mile away."

Is that why her nose is so long? Mia wondered. *For smelling lies?* It seemed like something a witch might be able to do. Mia decided not to take any chances. "I was talking to a fairy," she answered honestly.

"A fairy?" Mrs. Peavy made a sour face. "What nonsense!"

"But it's true!" Mia said. "She's right here!"

"What nonsense!" the woman repeated. "You must be a very silly girl."

"It's no use talking to her," Rosetta said, flying up next to Mia. "Most grown-ups can't see me. You can't see fairies if you don't believe in them."

How sad, Mia thought, *not to be able to see magic even when it's right in front of your eyes.* Suddenly, Mrs. Peavy didn't seem like a witch. She just seemed like a lonely old woman. A very *grouchy* lonely old woman.

"Now," Mrs. Peavy was saying, "what are you going to do about my hollyhocks?"

She pointed at the fence, where a row of unkempt hollyhocks grew. Mia saw that where she'd come through, she'd knocked over a few of the tall flowers. "You'll have to pay for them," her neighbor said.

"But I don't have any money!" Mia exclaimed.

"Then you'll have to work it off," said Mrs. Peavy, folding her arms.

Moments later, Mia found herself kneeling on the ground, pulling up weeds in Mrs. Peavy's garden. "This is terrible!" Mia whispered to Rosetta. "It will take a hundred years to weed this garden. We're never going to find Gabby. Or get you home again."

"This is my fault," said Rosetta. "If only she would go away!" She frowned at Mrs. Peavy, who was sitting on the patio, watching Mia like a hawk.

"You missed a spot!" the old woman called as the phone inside her home started to ring. She got up to answer it.

"It's about time!" Rosetta declared. Without wasting another moment, she began to fly in circles. As she did, the garden started to change.

Weeds shrank. Leaves sprouted. Brown grass turned green again. Wilted flowers straightened and burst into bloom. Round and round Rosetta went, leaving a trail of beauty in her wake. When the entire garden had been transformed,

Rosetta flew back to Mia. "There," she said, dusting off her hands. "That's much better."

Just then, Mrs. Peavy returned from the house. "I hope you've been pulling up weeds, not— What on earth?"

She froze at the sight of her beautiful garden and Mia standing in its midst.

"I'm finished, Mrs. Peavy," Mia said cheerily. When the woman didn't reply, she added, "I'll just let myself out the gate."

Mia left her neighbor staring in awe, the frown at last wiped clear off her face.

Chapter 7

When Mia and Rosetta returned to the house, they found Kate and Lainey still waiting in the backyard. Lainey was biting her nails. Kate was pacing the length of the fence like a tiger in a zoo.

"What took you so long?" Lainey cried when she saw them.

"We thought for sure the witch got you," Kate added.

"She's not a witch," Mia told them. "She's just a cranky old lady who needed a little bit of magic." She looked at Rosetta, who winked.

"While you were gone, we found something," Lainey reported. She pointed at one of the fence boards. "The nails here are a different color. They're new!"

"It must be the board your dad fixed," Kate explained. "That means it's the one that leads to Pixie Hollow!"

"Good work, guys," Mia said, picking up the hammer. She felt bad to be undoing her father's work. But what other choice did she have?

Mia was just working the hammer under the edge of the nail when the growl of a lawn mower made her jump. She turned to see her father pushing their mower around the side of the house.

Rosetta clapped her hands over her

ears. "What is that thing? It's louder than a bullfrog with a bellyache!"

"A lawn mower!" Kate shouted back. "It's for cutting the grass!"

Rosetta made a face. "All that fuss? Over a lawn's haircut?"

"Mia!" her father yelled. He said something else, but the sound of the mower drowned out the rest.

"What?" Mia cried.

Mr. Vasquez cut the motor. "I've got to mow the lawn. You girls need to play somewhere else for now." He looked around. "Where's Gabby?"

The girls all spoke at once.

"In the bathroom."

"Hiding."

"Upstairs."

"She's hiding in the bathroom upstairs,"

Mia said quickly. "We're, er, playing hide-and-seek."

"You'll have to finish your game inside. At least until I'm done out here." Her father reached down and started the mower again.

The girls trudged inside. They watched from the kitchen window as Mia's father pushed the mower back and forth. "At this rate, we'll never get back to Never Land," Kate complained.

On the windowsill, Rosetta was worried. "Isn't there some way we can stop it?" she asked Mia.

Mia shook her head. "Once he starts mowing the lawn, he always finishes. Except . . ."

"Except what?" asked Lainey.

"Well, I was just thinking of one time

when I left a jump rope on the lawn," Mia explained. "Papi didn't see it and mowed right over it. The mower jammed. He had to spend the rest of the day fixing it."

"That's what we can do!" Kate said. "We'll jam the mower!"

"No," Mia said firmly. "That's too dangerous. Papi said so. He was really mad last time. But maybe there's another way we can stop it."

Lainey was leaning out the window and studying the mower. "What's that bag on the back for?" she asked.

"It catches all the grass clippings," Mia said.

"That's what I thought," Lainey said. "Well, what if there was a little hole in the bag. He'd have to stop and fix that, right?"

"So you're saying *we* should put a hole in the bag?" Mia thought about it. "It's not a bad idea."

"Don't you think he'd see us doing something like that?" Kate asked.

"He'd see us," Mia said. "But he wouldn't see Rosetta." The girls all turned to the fairy.

Rosetta's eyes widened. "Oh no, not me! I'm a garden fairy. Holes aren't one of my talents, remember?"

"Please, Rosetta!" Mia said. "We have to get Gabby back. Otherwise, who knows what will happen—the passage to Never Land might stay closed forever! You might never get home."

Rosetta looked from Mia to Lainey to Kate. "To think I went through all this trouble for a pretty dress. Okay, I'll do it," she said with a sigh.

The girls decided that Mia should distract her father while Rosetta made the hole. Mia found a pair of nail scissors in a bathroom drawer. They were small enough for the tiny fairy to carry.

"Be careful," Mia said as she held them out to Rosetta.

Rosetta said nothing, but she took the scissors. Clutching them against her chest, she flew out the kitchen window into the backyard.

After Rosetta was in place, Mia went out the back door. "Papi!" she shouted.

When her father turned to her, she held up a glass of lemonade. "I thought you might need something to drink."

Her father cut the motor. "Well, that's very nice of you, Mia," he said, taking the glass. Over his shoulder, Mia could see Kate and Lainey watching. But where was Rosetta?

Then Mia spotted her. The fairy was perched on a tulip at the edge of the flower bed.

Why doesn't she go? Mia wondered. Then she noticed the flower trembling. She realized— Rosetta was scared!

Go, Rosetta, go! Mia silently urged.

After what seemed like an eternity, Rosetta lifted off the flower. She began to fly slowly toward them.

Mr. Vasquez finished the lemonade in two big gulps. He handed the glass back to Mia.

"Wait!" Mia cried, stalling for time. "Um . . . don't you want some more?"

"Not right now, thanks," her father said. "Maybe when I'm done." He reached down to start the mower.

With a jerk of the cord, the motor roared to life. Her father grabbed the handle of the mower and began to push.

Where was Rosetta? Mia couldn't see her. Had she made the hole? She glanced at the kitchen window. Kate's mouth was a round O. Lainey had her hands over her eyes.

Just then, Mia saw Rosetta. She was clinging to the mower bag as if for dear life. Then Mia's father turned the mower, and Rosetta disappeared from view.

Mia gasped.

Suddenly, a plume of grass clippings shot from the bag like a stream of smoke. Rosetta flew around the side of the mower. She smiled and waved at Mia.

Mia's heart gave a leap. She'd done it!

"What the—" Mia's father stopped the mower. He bent to examine the bag. Then, grumbling and shaking his head, he rolled the lawn mower back toward the garage.

Now was their chance! Rosetta flew over to Mia, and Kate and Lainey hurried outside. The girls met by the fence board.

"Way to go, Rosetta!" Mia said.

"That was cool," Kate agreed. She picked up the hammer, knelt down, and began to pry at the nail.

"Hurry, Kate!" Mia crossed her fingers. "If we get Gabby back before Mami comes home, I swear I'll never fight with her again."

"I've . . . almost . . . got it!" Kate pulled

the nail free, and the board swung sideways.

"Gabby!" Mia cried, leaning through the fence. "Gabby, we're here—"

Mia broke off. Pixie Hollow wasn't there. Once again, Mia found herself staring at Mrs. Peavy's backyard. She knew they'd found the right board this time. But the way back to Never Land was gone!

chapter 8

Iridessa scanned the trees, searching for a landmark—a twisted branch, an oddly shaped leaf, *anything* familiar. But in the growing gloom, one tree looked the same as the next.

Iridessa was furious with herself. How could she have gotten lost? And how could she have come into the forest so unprepared—without food or her basket of sunbeams or even a daisy umbrella to stay dry? It was unlike her to do anything without a plan.

It's because of Gabby, Iridessa thought. *I let myself get distracted.* Oh, if only she hadn't agreed to look after her!

But there was nothing she could do about it now. She had to get them both out of the forest.

She fanned her wings and was relieved to discover that they had dried. She fluttered off Gabby's shoulder, where she'd been riding. "Let's hurry," Iridessa urged. "The way back must be somewhere around here."

Gabby didn't seem to hear her. She stopped to pick another dandelion.

"Come along now, Gabby," Iridessa tried again. "We haven't got time to waste.

It will be getting dark soon."

Despite the thick clouds, Iridessa could tell that the sun was lower in the sky. The day was passing quickly, and she did not want to spend the night in the forest.

Gabby blew all the seeds off the dandelion, then threw the stem away. "I'm hungry," she said.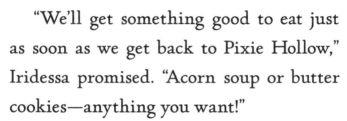

"We'll get something good to eat just as soon as we get back to Pixie Hollow," Iridessa promised. "Acorn soup or butter cookies—anything you want!"

"I want something now." A whine crept into Gabby's voice. To Iridessa's dismay, she suddenly sat down.

"We can't stop!" Iridessa wailed. But the girl refused to budge.

Desperately, Iridessa looked around.

Her eyes lit on a bush a short distance away. It was dotted with tiny fruit. *Blueberries!*

Relieved, Iridessa flew over and plucked two berries from the bush. She handed one to Gabby. Then she settled onto a tuffet of moss to eat the other one.

As Iridessa bit into the berry, sweet juice filled her mouth. She closed her eyes. *Mmm, that's good!* She hadn't realized how hungry she was. Quickly, she gobbled up the rest.

Iridessa patted her full stomach. Then she caught Gabby's eye. The girl was watching her longingly. It would take more than a single blueberry to fill up a hungry Clumsy, Iridessa realized.

She led Gabby to the berry bush and hovered anxiously as Gabby ate her fill.

Just as Gabby finished, there was another clap of thunder. The rain began to fall again.

This time they found shelter in a mossy hollow log. As they huddled together, Iridessa stared out at the rain. She was tired, cold, dirty, and damp. She didn't know what to do. The other fairies were all so busy, Iridessa knew it would be at least another day before anyone thought to look for them.

"Tell me a story, Iridessa," Gabby said, looking out at the rain.

"We haven't got time for—" Iridessa broke off. Right now, time was all they had. They couldn't go anywhere until the rain stopped. She searched her brain for a story but found only worries. "I can't

think of one. Why don't you tell me a story instead?"

"All right." Gabby thought for a moment. "Once upon a time, there was a fairy who lived in a place called Pixie Hollow."

"What was the fairy's name?" asked Iridessa.

"Iridessa," Gabby said without any hesitation.

Iridessa smiled. "That's a good name."

"Iridessa was friends with a girl," Gabby went on. "They were very best friends. They did all sorts of stuff together."

"What kinds of stuff?" Iridessa asked.

"Like once when they went into the woods. At first the girl was a little bit scared because it was dark, but then Iridessa showed her firefly magic. And when they got hungry, Iridessa made a blueberry bush grow."

"I didn't—" Iridessa stopped. It was just a story, after all. "Then what happened?"

Gabby yawned. "Um . . . then they

went home and had hot chocolate," she murmured. Her eyelids were growing heavy. "The end."

The rain drummed on the hollow log above them. Iridessa felt herself getting sleepy, too. She brightened her glow to try to stay awake. "Everything will be okay, Gabby," she said. "We'll get home soon."

"I know," Gabby said as her eyes closed. "Because you have fairy magic." A moment later, she was asleep.

Iridessa sat watching her. She had never known anyone, fairy or Clumsy, who had so much faith in fairy magic. Gabby thought Iridessa could do anything.

If only it were true, Iridessa thought. *If only I had the right magic to help us now.*

chapter 9

Warm sunlight touched Iridessa's face. She opened her eyes. She was lying at the entrance to the hollow log. Outside, the rain had stopped. Rays of morning sunlight shone down through the trees, making the wet forest sparkle.

Iridessa sat up quickly. She remembered that they were lost. *How could I have fallen asleep?* She turned to wake Gabby. But the log was empty.

Iridessa flew outside. She spotted the

little girl a short distance away. Gabby was staring at something in the trees.

She smiled as Iridessa flew up to her. "Look," she said, pointing.

A trail of dandelions led through the forest. All Gabby's wishes hadn't been for nothing after all, Iridessa realized. They had left a path of seeds behind them—and after the rain, the flowers had sprouted. Their yellow dandelion heads pointed the way home. There must have been some magic in those wishes for the flowers to sprout so quickly, Iridessa thought.

"Oh, you clever girl!" Iridessa cried. *All this time I thought I was taking care of Gabby,* she mused. *But really, she's been taking care of me.*

"If we hurry, we'll be back in time for breakfast," Iridessa said. "Come on, Gabby. I'll race you!"

Iridessa and Gabby arrived back in Pixie Hollow to find everything ready for a party. Colorful paper lanterns hung from the branches of the Home Tree. Walnuts roasted on spits over tiny fires, and vats of honeysuckle punch stood around the courtyard. The sound of musicians tuning their finger harps drifted through the air.

Iridessa's first thought was that Pixie Hollow was holding a party to welcome them home. Then she realized—the fairies must have finished fixing the bridge during the night. The party was to celebrate the bridge's reopening.

"Ah, home!" Iridessa exclaimed. The smell of the walnuts made her mouth water. "Come on. Let's get something to eat."

Gabby didn't reply. She looked around with a forlorn expression. Suddenly, a tear rolled down her cheek.

"What's wrong?" Iridessa asked in surprise.

"My wish didn't come true," Gabby said, then burst into tears.

Iridessa had been so happy to be back that she'd forgotten about Gabby's problem. Now she remembered how far the girl was from her own home. "Did you wish the hole would be fixed?" she asked gently.

"No." Gabby sniffled. "I wished Mia wouldn't be mad at me anymore. I wished she would be right here in Pixie Hollow waiting for me. But she didn't come. She doesn't care about me."

"Oh, Gabby, of course she does," Iridessa said.

Gabby shook her head. "She says I mess everything up."

"You don't mess everything up," Iridessa said. "You're the one who got us back to Pixie Hollow. And you rescued me from the flood. And you're the one who found all the fireflies in the forest. You did everything right. You are sweet and brave and imaginative. I would be glad if you were my sister."

Iridessa realized that it was true. If it weren't for Gabby, she never would have seen the dancing fireflies or the trail of wishes. Those things hadn't been part of her plan, but Iridessa wouldn't have wanted to miss them for the world.

Gabby had her own kind of magic, she thought. And in its way, it was as powerful as any fairy magic.

But Iridessa's words didn't seem to comfort Gabby. The tears continued to trickle down her face.

Nearby, a silver dandelion was growing in the grass. Gabby halfheartedly plucked it and blew away its seeds. "I want to go home," she said.

*

On the other side of the fence, Mia clutched her head. "It didn't work!" she cried. "Why didn't it work?"

"Let me try," Kate said. She swung the board shut, then pulled it open again. But all they saw was the neighbor's yard.

"So I can't ever get home again." Rosetta slumped. In the wrinkled doll's dress, she looked like a wilted flower. Mia felt terrible. Just a few hours before, it had seemed like so much fun to have a fairy living in her dollhouse. But now that it was about to come true, it felt like a tragedy.

Tears pricked Mia's eyes. "I'm so sorry, Rosetta. It's all my fault. I never should have brought you here. I should have been watching Gabby."

Mia thought of Gabby that morning. How she'd wanted to play a game. *If only I'd played with her!* Mia thought. Now she might never have the chance to play with her sister again.

Mia wasn't worried about getting in trouble with her parents. She wasn't thinking of how she'd tell Gabby off. She just wanted her sister back.

Through the screen of her tears, Mia saw something white drifting through the air. *Snowflakes—in summertime?* Mia wiped her eyes. But then she saw that they weren't snowflakes after all. They were dandelion seeds.

Lainey and Kate noticed them, too. "Where did those come from?" Kate wondered.

Rosetta caught one of the silky seeds. She pressed it to her ear, and her eyes widened. "This seed is from Never Land!"

Mia leaped to her feet. "Are you sure? How do you know?"

Rosetta lifted her chin. "I told you, I can hear the secrets inside a seed. It's what garden fairies do."

More dandelion seeds drifted down through the air. Mia looked up and saw that they were coming from Gabby's open bedroom window.

The girls all looked at each other.

"Do you think . . . ?" Kate began.

"That the hole moved?" Lainey nodded. "It's possible."

"Anything is possible in Never Land," Mia agreed.

The girls raced into the house, with Rosetta flying behind. Mia took the stairs two at a time. When she opened the door to Gabby's room, she saw dandelion seeds drifting from beneath the closet door.

Mia held her breath, hardly daring to hope. She put her hand on the doorknob.

When she pulled the door open, she felt a warm breeze against her face. She smelled orange blossoms and sun-warmed moss.

Mia stepped through the door, crying, "Gabby! We're coming!"

chapter 10

As Mia went through the dark closet, she had a moment of doubt. What if the opening had moved on the Never Land side, too? What if it led to a pirate's ship or a dragon's lair rather than Pixie Hollow?

But a second later, Mia and her friends emerged into sunlight. They were standing on the bank of Havendish Stream. From across the stream, they could hear the lively sound of fairy music.

"I'm home! Oh, it's so good to be back!"

Rosetta exclaimed. She did a joyous twirl in the air, then darted away without a backward glance.

She didn't even say good-bye, thought Mia. But she didn't have time to dwell on that. For just ahead, standing in the Home Tree courtyard, was her sister.

"Gabby!" Mia splashed through the stream, not caring that her feet got wet. A moment later, she had her wrapped in a hug so tight that she lifted Gabby right off the ground.

"You came!" Gabby exclaimed, hugging her sister back.

"Of course I came!" Mia said. "We've been trying to get here all day."

"So you're not mad at me?" Gabby asked as Mia set her down.

"Mad? I'm furious with you!" Mia

exclaimed, giving her sister another big hug. This time Kate and Lainey joined in.

"I thought you closed the hole because you were mad at me," Gabby said.

"What? No!" Mia laughed. "We couldn't get here because Papi fixed the fence."

"And when we got the board loose again, the hole was gone!" Lainey explained.

"But you'll never believe where it showed up!" Kate jumped in. "*Your* room, Gabby! You're so lucky. You can go to Never Land anytime you want, day or night."

"No she can't!" Mia said quickly. "You're not allowed to go to Never Land without me."

"Or me," said Kate.

"Or me," added Lainey. "But I still don't understand why the hole moved."

"Never Land must want you here," Iridessa suddenly spoke up.

All the girls turned to the fairy, who was hovering next to Gabby. "What do you mean? Never Land is just an island," Kate pointed out. "How can it want something?"

"It's an island with a mind of its own," Iridessa said. "Have you ever heard the expression 'When one knothole closes, another one opens'?"

"It's 'when one *door* closes, another one opens,'" Lainey said.

"Door. Knothole." Iridessa shrugged. "Never Land must have opened a path for you to reach it. It's the only explanation I can think of."

Mia noticed how Iridessa hovered near Gabby's shoulder. She didn't seem to want to leave her side. Mia was about to ask what Never Land wanted them for, but at that moment, Rosetta came flying back. Tinker Bell was with her.

"I told Tink all about the grass machine and the hole I put in it," she said. "She thinks she can fix it."

Tinker Bell looked excited. "It sounds like an interesting case."

"It didn't seem right to leave it for your father to fix," Rosetta explained.

"Are you sure it's a good idea to come back with us?" Mia asked. "What if the hole closes again, and you get stuck like Rosetta did?"

Tink puffed her chest out bravely. "I've been to the mainland before. I can manage."

"But you must stay for the bridge-opening party!" Rosetta clapped her hands. "A party at last! I wonder what I should wear?" She looked down at the doll's dress, which was looking bedraggled after her adventure on the mainland. "It's a shame about this one, after all that trouble."

"We can't stay for the party. What about your mom?" Lainey reminded Mia.

"Oh! That's right. Mami is coming home any minute. We have to get back right away!" Mia grabbed Gabby's hand.

Gabby dug in her heels. "No, I want to stay."

"Gabby . . . ," Mia warned. And just like that, the two began arguing again.

At last, Mia convinced Gabby to go home, swearing that they would return to Pixie Hollow as soon as they could. They said their good-byes to Rosetta and Iridessa. Then, with Tink flying alongside them, the girls headed back to the hollow tree.

Before she ducked inside, Mia turned for one last look at Pixie Hollow. She took in the flowers, the music, and the beautiful Home Tree, trying to tuck it all away in her memory. Mia was sure that they would be back—almost sure, anyway. But she wanted to remember everything, just in case.

Then Mia turned toward the hole that led back home. As she stepped through, she took Gabby's hand tightly in her own.

Read this Sneak peek of Under the lagoon, the newest Never Girls adventure!

Gabby Vasquez soared through the sky over Never Land. The wind blew her hair off her forehead. It whipped the cloth wings on her back, making them flutter like real fairy wings.

Gabby spread her arms wide. She loved flying! Up here she could be anything. She was a giant, with clouds as her ceiling and the forest as her floor. She was the queen of the world! She was—

"Gabby!" Her sister's voice cut through her thoughts.

Gabby looked back. Mia was flying behind her, along with their friends Kate McCrady and Lainey Winters. The fairy Tinker Bell was with them.

"Slow down," Mia called. "You'll miss the turn!"

"No, I won't!" Gabby yelled back. But she slowed down. Together the girls and Tink banked right. As they came up over a crest, a beautiful blue-green lagoon came into view. Looking down, Gabby's heart skipped a beat. They were there!

Mermaids!

They sat together, fanning their tails and combing their beautiful long hair. Gabby waved to them. The mermaids shaded their eyes and looked up as she passed. But none of them waved back.

The girls and Tink started their descent toward the beach. As Gabby landed, she stumbled in the sand and almost fell. She glanced up quickly to see if the mermaids had noticed. But they were already sliding into the water. Gabby saw the tips of their tails as they slipped beneath the surface.

"They're doing it again!" she cried.

"Who's doing what?" asked Tinker Bell.

"The mermaids! Why do they dive whenever we come? Are they afraid of us?" Gabby asked.

Tink looked at the lagoon. It was empty now. Not so much as a ripple showed that mermaids had ever been there. "No, they're not afraid," Tink said.

"Then why?"

"They're not interested in us," Tink said with a shrug.

"Why not?" asked Gabby. "*I'm* interested in *them*."

"Trust me, it's better this way," said Tink. "They're not the nicest creatures in Never Land."

Gabby had heard other fairies say this about mermaids, but she never understood why. After all, mermaids were beautiful and magical, like fairies. To Gabby, it made sense that they should all be friends.

"There must be *some* nice mermaids," she said. But Tink had already turned away.

"We're not here to see mermaids, anyway," Mia said. She was helping Lainey pull a deflated raft out of the bushes. "We're here to see *Sunny*."

Sunny was Lainey's pet goldfish—at least, he *had* been Lainey's pet before she'd accidentally set him free in Never Land and he'd grown—and grown and *grown*. Now her goldfish was as big as a golden retriever! Lainey couldn't keep him anymore, so he lived in the Mermaid Lagoon. The girls visited him when they could, using a raft they'd brought from Mia and Gabby's house.

"First we need to get the raft fixed. There's a hole somewhere," Lainey said, showing the sagging raft to Tinker Bell. Tink was good at fixing things.

Tink flew around the raft, stopping now and then to press one pointed ear against it, until she found the leak. While Tink patched the hole, Gabby walked around the beach, collecting seashells. There were more—and more interesting—shells here than on any other beach she'd visited. Gabby found several pink scalloped shells, a purple shell shaped like a pincushion, and a long, twisty shell that looked like a unicorn's horn. She put them all in the pocket of her sweatshirt.

A little farther down the beach, she found a bright orange starfish. Turning it over in her hands, Gabby felt a thrill of excitement. She'd seen mermaids wearing starfish in their hair. Maybe this one belonged to a mermaid, too! She imagined the mermaid searching everywhere for her missing hairpiece. How happy she would be if Gabby gave it back! *"It's lucky I found it,"* Gabby imagined herself saying. *"I knew*

you would miss it." And then the mermaid would say—

"Come on, Gabby!"

"What?" Gabby blinked out of her daydream. Mia, Kate, and Lainey were looking at her.

"The raft is fixed. We're ready to go," Mia said.

"I want to stay here," Gabby said. The truth was, she didn't really like visiting Sunny. He'd been cute when he was a little goldfish. But now that he was almost as big as she was, Gabby found him kind of scary.

Mia's brow furrowed. "But we can't leave you alone."

Why did Mia always have to baby her?

Excerpt from *Under the Lagoon* copyright © 2016 by Disney Enterprises, Inc. Published in the United States by Random House Children's Books, a division of Penguin Random House LLC, New York.